KILLER ON FIRE

KILLER TRILOGY BOOK 3

ALEXIS ABBOTT

PATHFORGERS PUBLISHING

Get an EXCLUSIVE book, **FREE** just as a thank you for signing up for my newsletter! Plus you'll never miss a new release, cover reveal, or promotion!

http://alexisabbott.com/newsletter

He said he'd always keep me safe.

He told me everything would be okay in the end. He promised me that no matter what happened, we would face it together. Side by side. Hand in hand. Luca and Serena, us against the world. After everything we've been through, it was easy to think we could overcome all odds and emerge victorious together. Love conquers all, doesn't it?

He told me so. And I believed him.

Is this cruel world going to make a liar out of the love of my life?

Almost like an answer, the car jostles and thumps over a pothole in the road, causing the seatbelt to strain against my barely-pregnant belly. I instinctively lay my hands over my stomach. As though that might be enough to protect the child I'm carrying. As if I have any control over what happens to my baby and me anymore. A lump forms in my throat, aching as I force myself to swallow down another dry sob. I'm all cried out. In fact, I'm probably pretty dehydrated from crying for so long. How long, exactly, I'm not sure. Time stopped for me the moment that car bomb exploded. The hours stopped making sense when Nico threw Rafaela and me into his car and sped away from the scene of the crime.

All I know is that I've been in a car—various cars, actually—for what feels like an eternity. Hours and hours, probably. I've lost count of how many times I've switched off into a different car, with a different driver. I don't know where I am or where I'm going. The scenery outside my window, dimly lit by street-lights and the crescent moon, all blends together into nothingness. I can't make the world around me make sense, not without Luca by my side.

He's all I can think about. It feels like there's a massive, gaping hole in my heart, and I can't find the missing piece to make it complete again. I'm trying to figure out what led me to this moment. How the hell did I get here? Alone and afraid and broken-hearted? I've replayed the scene a thousand times in my head: the hail of bullets, the explosion, the flash of bright light, the smell of burning metal and rubber. Nico pushing me to the ground to shield me from attack. Rafaela sobbing. The screams of the crowd, the bodies dropping in the street.

The sight of what used to be Luca's car, now a mass of flame and smoke, shrinking smaller and smaller on the horizon in the rear view mirror as we drove away and left the man I love behind in the impossible wreckage. Not a single sign of life. Nothing at all to give me some tiny glittering bead of hope that Luca might have survived. I kept waiting for that sign, long after the burning car was out of sight. I expected Nico to assure me that Luca was just going to the hospital. That he was hurt, but alive.

But it didn't. Nothing happened. Nothing changed. That sign never came.

Nico drove for a long while. Rafaela finally stopped crying and we rode in silence. I was too shocked to even speak, just staring down at my hands. The ring sparkling on my finger. After an hour or so, Nico spoke up. He informed me solemnly that he was taking me to a drop point, where I would be transferred to another vehicle for the next leg of my getaway journey. I didn't even respond. There was nothing to say. Sure, I could have asked where they would take me, where I would end up, who was going to look after me, how long I would have to be gone. Was this going to be permanent? What would happen to the baby? Would we just start over? Begin a quiet new life somewhere far away, try to forget the horrors I've witnessed?

But honestly? I didn't care. Not then. Not right after watching the love of my life be devoured by greedy flames. Watching my whole heart, my future reduced to ash.

I have hardly noticed the faces of the many men who have driven me all this way. There were so many pass-overs, so many cars... They're trying to be secure, and every couple of hours, I have to shift from one vehicle to the next, in a daze.

I haven't even noticed which direction we're going. I couldn't tell you the make and model or even the color of the vehicles I've been traveling in for the past half-day or so. It doesn't matter anyway. Wherever I end up, it'll all be the same. Without Luca, there is no safe place to go. There is no hope anymore.

I've stayed pretty much silent all this time, except for when necessity made me speak up and ask the driver to pull over so I could throw up. I don't know if it's pregnancy nausea or just my body reacting to the horrific scene I keep replaying in my head, but my stomach just won't settle. I haven't eaten for hours, and I've barely touched a drop of the bottled water Nico shoved into my purse before passing me onto the next driver. I know, deep down, eventually I will have to give in and start acting like a person again. If not for my sake, then for the baby's sake. But right now, I just can't bring myself to care.

When these current drivers took me into their car, they made me turn my phone off just in case the Cleaners might somehow tap my phone or track it. But after a while, I surreptitiously turned it back on. The threat of being tracked down by the bad guys doesn't scare me like it probably should. It seems more important to have my phone on. Just in case. I keep thinking my phone will buzz with a text message.

Mia passerotta, not even death can take me from you.

I swallow hard and check my phone for the hundredth time. Nothing. Of course.

"Take this exit," says the stocky guy in the passenger seat. The driver nods. I finally look out the window and catch a glimpse of the sun rising through the clouds. The sky is streaked pink and orange, casting a beautiful peachy glow over the highway, the trees lining the pavement. We're crossing state lines, heading west, I think. Maybe south? Not that it matters.

My stomach lurches again and I clap a hand over my mouth as I feel the bile rising up my throat. Ugh. Not again. I struggle to gain some composure for a moment, and then lean forward to tap the guy in the passenger seat on his muscular shoulder.

"Sir," I murmur, my voice sounding rough from the hours of crying. He turns to look at me with mild surprise, almost like he's forgotten I've been back here the whole time. "Could you guys pull over somewhere? I think I'm gonna be sick again."

"You got food poisoning or somethin'?" he asks, raising an eyebrow. The driver reaches across the console to shove him on the arm.

"She's pregnant, you prick," says the driver, his voice low and gruff. "Remember?"

The stocky guy makes a face halfway between a grimace and a wince. "Oh. Well, what the hell do we want with a pregnant lady—"

The driver reaches over and punches him in the arm before he can finish the sentence. I roll my eyes and rest my forehead against the window, trying not to vomit all over the swanky leather interior of this getaway car. The trees flashing by are making me feel sicker, my head spinning. I close my eyes and just try to focus on breathing slowly. In and out. In and out.

After a few minutes of gradually slowing down, the vehicle pulls onto a shoulder and rolls to a stop. I hurriedly push open the door and run as fast as my cramped legs can carry me to the edge of where the woodsy brush begins to keel over and vomit. Once I'm done, I hobble weakly back to the car, finally use some of that bottled water to rinse my mouth out, and settle into my seat again. I click the seatbelt over my chest, a hand cradling my barely-there baby bump. As the car pulls back onto the road, the passenger-side guy turns around and offers me a stick of minty gum.

"Might help ya feel a little less gross," he says, shrugging. I take the gum thankfully.

As I'm chewing it, I happen to glance up at the rear view mirror and notice the driver staring at me. As soon as we make eye contact, his eyes flick back to the road. Weird, but then again, I suppose it's not every day these guys have to transport a random pregnant girl across state lines.

Especially if they know what kind of shit I'm running from.

It's not like these Costa guys know how to comfort a grieving, emotional, hormonal woman. Stuff like this is probably not high on their list of priorities, and I can't imagine their training prepares them for a situation like mine.

A stupid thought pops up in my head: *they're more afraid of you than you are of them.* If I wasn't so depressed and numb, I might have laughed. But no sooner does this amusing thought appear than it disappears, and the image of Luca's face, smiling down at me at the celebratory dinner table last night swims to the front of my mind.

That handsome, strong face. Those sharp cheekbones. Those sensuous lips. Those olive-green eyes lit up with flames of love, burning brightly for me alone.

Now a different kind of flame is burning. My

eyes itch, wanting to cry but unable to pull any tears. There aren't any left. I feel my cheeks going red, my heart skipping a beat and that pit in my stomach as I remember that I will never get to see those beautiful eyes again. He's gone. Luca is gone, and I am all alone in the world.

Well, not quite alone. Luca may have left me, swallowed up by the fire, but I'm still here and this baby needs to have at least one parent alive. I know it's what Luca would want—for me to pull myself together for the sake of the child.

It would shatter his heart to think of me just giving up, throwing in the towel.

He would want me to be strong. This baby needs me to be strong. He or she is all that's left of Luca in the world, and if I were to just let my grief take over instead of keeping a brave face and doing what I have to do for our kid, what kind of wife would I be?

Sure, we never got to have a wedding. We were getting there. We thought we had time. Why in the world should we have expected things to fall apart so completely? Besides, even if we didn't make it official in time, I will always consider myself Luca's wife. I've been his all along.

My heart has belonged to Luca since I was sixteen years old, and that isn't going to change just because he's gone. No, I've got to hold it together somehow. For the baby. For Luca's memory.

Which means I need to drag myself out of this

darkness bit by bit. I need to remember who the hell I am. I will never, ever get over losing Luca. This pain is going to stay with me for the rest of my life. But if I let it dominate me completely, how can I be a good mother to our baby?

Nope.

I need a break from this constant mourning. A distraction, at least for a little while. Rubbing my stomach absentmindedly, I decide to distract myself and try to make conversation. The silence is getting a little awkward anyway.

"So where are you taking me?" I pipe up, barely able to even conjure enough energy to sound interested in the answer. But I'm trying.

The driver and passenger-seat guy look at each other for a moment without replying. I start to wonder if they even heard me. Then the stocky passenger says, "Uh, you know. South."

"South," I repeat flatly. That's not much of an answer. Suddenly, I *am* a little interested.

"Mhmm."

"Okay," I mumble, frowning. "Could you maybe be more specific?"

"You don't need to worry about the details," the driver interrupts. "We're handling everything. You just sit back and relax, alright?"

"Oh!" exclaims the passenger-seat guy suddenly. He opens the dash compartment and takes out a white medicine bottle, the pills rattling around inside. "You got a messed-up stomach, right? Well, I just remembered we got these pills here. You know. For motion sickness and shit."

I catch the driver smiling into the rear view mirror. It seems strange, somehow.

The stocky guy turns in his seat and offers me two oblong olive-colored pills. I cock my head to one side, a little confused. Something seems off. When I was a teenager, I used to have horrible motion sickness. Bad enough that our family doctor prescribed me clinical-strength meclizine for it so that I could ride the subway without turning green in the face.

And I have never seen motion sickness medicine that looks like that.

"Wh-what is it?" I ask, hesitantly reaching for the green pills.

"Uh, what's this shit called again, boss?" the stocky guy says.

"What's it—oh yeah, Dramamine. Yeah."

"Right, right. Dramamine. It's Dramamine."

The passenger-seat guy twists back to look at me over his shoulder, his eyes glancing down to see that I'm still just holding the pills in my hand. He waits expectantly for me to put them in my mouth, staring at me with beady black eyes.

"Whatcha waitin' for? Don't you wanna feel better?" he urges me.

Just as I'm second-guessing my paranoia, there's

a series of deafening cracks splitting the air, and a rain of shattered glass flies toward me from the left-side window. I scream and duck down, bending over my stomach and covering my head with my hands. The car jerks left, then right, hits a bump in the road, and starts spinning rapidly.

"Jesus Christ!"

"What the fuck was that?"

"Get your gun, get your gun!"

I close my eyes tightly and try not to throw up, my head swimming with dizziness as the vehicle careens out of control. There's a horrible whooshing sound as the car slides off the road, over the rumble strip, and thuds across the grass. I open my eyes just as another staccato cluster of gunshots rings out and a spray of bright red blood stains the dashboard. The driver's been shot!

The car rolls straight into a tree with a powerful thump. I'm flung forward, my head knocking into the center console with a nauseating crack. I feel my vision go dark and my body fall limp, all sound fading out into nothing behind the rhythmic thud of my heart.

When the light starts to filter back in and my head tingles as I wake back up, the passenger door swings open and a pair of powerful arms reach inside to yank me out of the back seat. I scream, thrashing and flailing with what limited strength my body can conjure up, fighting with my assailant. My vision is still blurry, my head pounding painfully, and I have no idea whose hands are on me right now. There's another gunshot, so close to me that my ears sting with a high-pitched ringing, rendering me both stunned and deaf and completely helpless.

"Let me go! Get your hands off me!" I screech, flinging knees and elbows in every direction, hoping I can somehow dislodge myself from my attacker's grasp. I don't have much of a plan beyond that.

I mean, I may be only barely starting to show, but I'm still pregnant. What am I going to do? Take off running into the woods? Still, the fact that it's not only my life in danger, but the life of my baby, makes me fight that much harder.

I'm fighting for two.

"Serena!" the guy says through gritted teeth. He knows my name? And not only that, he says it with some degree of familiarity. Like he knows me. It's so off-putting that I stop struggling for a moment and turn to look at him square in the face. He sighs, shaking his head. His eyes are wide, exhausted, with purplish bags under them. He looks like he hasn't slept for a long time.

I don't immediately recognize him. I squint, tilting my head to one side. Confusion and curiosity have overtaken my fear at this point. He doesn't seem malicious, at least towards me, despite the fact that he just shot my drivers and caused my getaway car to smash into a tree. Then it hits me. I've seen his face before, and recently.

"You were… you were at the party," I murmur, my words slurring. Wow, I must have really hit my head pretty hard. His face swims in front of me and I have to blink a few times to focus again. He nods and gently sets me aside, but with one hand still locked around my upper arm, as though I'm a wild animal he needs to keep on a leash.

"*Si.* Yeah, I was there, Serena. We met briefly," he admits, exhaling slowly. He stares at the ground for a second, then looks back up at me with mournful eyes. "I cannot even imagine what's going through your mind right now."

I can feel my bottom lip trembling, my cheeks burning, my eyes itching. This guy seems to know how crushed I am. And it starts to make some sense. If he was at that party, then he's got to be an old friend of Luca's or something. Maybe he's hurting, too. But then… why the hell would he have intercepted my escape?

My heart skips a beat and I feel nauseous again

all of a sudden. I whip around to look at the carnage behind us in the car. Glass shattered all over. The engine smoking profusely under the hood. Two men shot dead. Blood everywhere.

Instinctively I try to rip out of the guy's grasp, clapping a hand over my mouth and turning away.

But he doesn't let me go.

I give him a furious glare and snap, "If you don't let me go right now I am going to vomit all over your shoes."

He immediately releases his grip, but stays close behind me as I break away, running deeper into woods to throw up again. When I stand back up and turn around, I nearly bump smack into him. To his credit, he doesn't seem at all fazed by my sickness. But if he's the kind of dude who goes around shooting men in cars then, yeah, he's probably got a stronger stomach than most.

"A little space would be nice," I grumble, elbowing past him. He takes my arm again and I stamp my foot in annoyance. I do not like being manhandled.

"Okay, what's up with this? You better tell me why you just assassinated my... my getaway!" I demand.

He runs his other hand back through his curly black hair.

"My apologies. I have not slept much since... since what happened after the party."

"Yeah, well, you're not the only one," I retort, putting my free hand on my hip.

He nods slowly.

"I know. I know. It has been more difficult for you, I'm sure."

"So, any particular reason why you decided to smash up my getaway car and murder two guys in front of me?" I ask, surprised at my own bluntness. I'm usually a little more reserved than this, but it's like that numbness I was feeling earlier has gone away and left pure, righteous anger in its place. I'm finding it hard to give a shit about anything beyond getting some straight answers.

"Those men weren't Costa. Somewhere along the way, the Cleaners intercepted your route. Those two used to work for the Costa family, but they left. Went to the Cleaners. Fairly recently, too. Recent enough that the Costa brothers who passed you off to them just saw familiar faces in the dark and trusted them. They made a mistake. They'll be punished for that transgression," the guy says calmly, as though he's merely discussing the weather.

I, on the other hand, am terrified by what he's telling me.

"What?" I hiss, my eyes going wide. "You mean those guys—they weren't taking me to safety? They were going to hurt me? And-and my baby?"

"Kill you or ransom you both, most likely," he replies.

"Jesus," I mutter, wrapping an arm over my belly. I look up at him confusedly.

"Then how… how the hell did you find me?"

"Your phone," he says simply. "It was off for some time, but then it came back on. We followed the GPS tracker Lu—an associate installed a while back."

"You can say his name, you know," I tell him quietly. "You don't have to pretend like he never existed."

We stare at each in silence for a few intense moments, and I can feel the combined sadness between us. It hits me that the dark circles under his eyes probably have more to do with what happened to Luca than this multi-state car chase he's been on to catch me.

I break the silence. I have to, before it can swallow us both whole. "Speaking of names—you said we met at the party but I have to admit, I was a little overwhelmed there. I don't remember your name, I'm sorry."

"Giovanni," he says. "Luca and I are—were—very old friends."

There it is. The past tense. Out in the air, hanging there between us. I have to fight the urge to cry. Just break down, fall on my knees, and cry. But I can't. Not now. Not here. I have to stay strong. I just need to survive this day, and then...

Then what?

I honestly don't know. I just have to focus on one

step at a time. I just have to focus on the present mess I find myself in.

"What are we going to do about… all that?" I ask, gesturing back toward the wreckage behind us. Giovanni shrugs.

"*We* don't do anything. Our tidying-up team will be out here any second now to make this look more accidental than it was. You're very lucky," he adds as he leads me back to where his car is parked, a few hundred yards down the highway. "This time of early morning, there aren't many other cars around. And those guys were taking you down a very secluded route. Probably trying to avoid the cops. Kind of bit them in the ass in the end, though."

"Uh, yeah. I'd say so," I answer, raising an eyebrow.

Giovanni almost smiles for a moment, but it vanishes as quickly as it appeared. Once we get close to his car, the passenger-side door opens and a butch-looking woman comes hurrying over with a little white kit in her hand. There's a look of motherly concern on her face as she comes up to me.

"Serena, this is Orsina. She's a medic with the Costa family," Giovanni explains. Then to her, he adds, "Make it quick, if you can. The sun's up now and there will be traffic out here before too long. We need to get out of dodge."

Orsina nods at him and then gives me a kind, reassuring smile. "How are you feeling?" she asks.

"Did you sustain any major injuries in the crash? How's the little one doing in there?"

I shake my head. "I-I don't think I'm hurt, really. I did hit my head a little bit."

A flash of worry crosses her face, but the smile comes back quickly. "Okay, sweetheart, let's get you into the car. I'll tend to you in the back seat while Giovanni drives. He's right, we do need to get going. Are you feeling nauseous at all?"

I almost have to laugh at this question. Instead, I just nod as she helps me into the back seat of the car.

"Yeah, lots of nausea. But I was having that long before the car crashed."

Giovanni slides behind the wheel and starts the engine. The car quickly peels out and does a sharp U-turn, cutting across the grassy median and speeding off down the highway in the opposite direction of how I got here.

Orsina touches my arm softly.

"Serena, when was the last time you ate something?"

I have to wrack my brain for an answer to that. Truthfully, I don't remember much beyond the past hour or so. It's like my mind is desperately trying to cut out all the painful pieces so I don't have to think about them. I know I had to have eaten something at the party, but I can't remember.

"I-I don't know," I tell her honestly. And now, with this woman gazing concernedly into my face, the tears reemerge. My eyes tingle and my chin trembles. Before long, I'm full-on sobbing, and Orsina wraps her arms around me in a maternal hug, patting my back.

"I know, sweetheart. Just let it all out. If anybody on the planet has the right to a good cry right now, it's definitely you," she assures me. I weep on her shoulder for several minutes, all my emotions rushing back to me in a swarm of overwhelming feeling. Images flash to the forefront of my mind. Rafaela dancing and singing drunkenly in Spanish on the sidewalk. The streetlights casting fuzzy light over the street. The smile Luca gave me just before he walked away to get the car. The sky-high flames destroying the car with the love of my life trapped inside the inferno.

It's too much to bear. It's all too much. But I let the tears fall without trying to stop them. I take Orsina's advice and let it all out, not caring about how my tears are staining her shirt, how ugly my sobs sound, how weak I must look to both of them. It doesn't matter. I need this.

And when the tears subside, Orsina gently starts to dab a clean rag dampened with hydrogen peroxide at my left temple, near my hairline. It stings, to my surprise, and I let out a little yelp of pain.

"Oh, I'm sorry, sweetie," Orsina says, clucking her tongue. "You just have a little wound here from the impact. Nothing too awful, just a relatively shallow laceration. Could be much, much worse. I know you don't feel too lucky right now, but you are."

"People keep telling me that," I murmur, the dizziness rushing back and mingling with the pain in my head. A throbbing ache settles in and I close my eyes, leaning back against the seat. As soon as I do, my whole body relaxes, like one big sigh. It hits me how tense I've been all this time, how tired I feel underneath all the stress.

"Here," the medic says, "hold this rag to the spot for a minute while I get a bandage ready. Can you do that for me, Serena?"

I nod and obediently hold the rag to my temple. There's a plasticky sound of something being unwrapped, and then Orsina takes the rag away, replacing it with a big bandage. She presses it down carefully, obviously trying her best not to hurt me, but every little feather-light touch stings like hell. Still, I almost welcome the sting. Physical pain is a lot easier to understand, to handle, than the ache in my heart.

"There ya go," Orsina says. "Now just leave that alone and it should heal up okay. Probably won't even leave a scar, if your luck holds out."

"Thank you," I mumble, suddenly feeling very sleepy. It's like the tidal wave of emotions has crashed over me and exhausted every last little fiber of my strength. I'm worn out, down to the very bone, with fear and sadness and confusion.

Then Giovanni speaks up and I open my eyes one at a time. "We had planned on sending you to a safehouse in backwoods Virginia. Somewhere out of the way and secure. But if your getaway was already compromised so early in the game… well, it's probably best to scrap Plan A and just move on to Plan B."

I can feel myself dozing off. "What's… what's Plan B?" I manage to whisper.

But I drift off to sleep before I can hear the answer.

~

I wake up to the sensation of being jostled forward, and my eyes fly open and wide. I sit up with a start, blinking blearily in the bright light of day. I'm still in the back seat of the car, with Orsina the medic sitting next to me. But the car isn't moving anymore. We've stopped.

The driver's seat is empty, and then the door to my left opens up and Giovanni extends a hand for me to take. Orsina gets out of the car and comes around to help him help me. I squint around, trying to make sense of my environment. My body is so tired, and that familiar nausea is prickling back up again, warning me that any sudden movement might send me hurling.

We're in the middle of what looks like deep woods. I remember vaguely Giovanni mentioning something about the backwoods of Virginia, but then I put together what he said: Virginia was Plan A, and we weren't going to do Plan A anymore. Unless he changed his mind?

"Where... where the hell are we?" I ask, the words jumbling in my mouth.

There isn't an immediate answer. Orsina and Giovanni are helping me down a long wooded path through the trees. My paranoia kicks back in and I plant my feet hard in the ground, refusing to take another step.

"Where. The hell. Are we?" I repeat emphatically, looking back and forth between the two of them. They exchange a worrisome expression, and I know something is up. Something I am not going to like one bit. "Enough with the secrecy! What's going on? I thought you said we were ditching the Virginia plan!" I exclaim.

"Yes. You're right. We're on to Plan B," Giovanni relents.

"Okay. Cool. Great. So what *is* Plan B?" I ask, crossing my arms over my chest.

Orsina steps closer to me and puts a steadying hand on my shoulder. "Sweetheart, you're going to overexert yourself. It's okay. You can trust us. You know that, right? You're not with the Cleaners anymore. You're with us. You're with family."

"Family?" I repeat, a little indignant. After all, I don't really know these people. Maybe Luca knew them, but he's gone now, and it's up to me to stay level-headed and cautious for the sake of our baby. They don't want me asking questions, clearly, and that scares me.

Giovanni sighs.

"Yes, Serena. I know you have been through so much in the past day or so. It's a lot to take in. But you have to trust us. From the second Luca fell in love with you, we became your family. If he trusted you, if he swore to protect you, then so do we. There is no safer place in the world for you to be than with us. Especially now that Luca's… gone. We want nothing more than to continue the work Luca was doing, and that involves you. And the baby. You're safe with us. I can promise you that."

"Everything is up in the air right now. I know it's hard. This time has been difficult for all of us. Luca was well-loved," Orsina interjects, her voice soft and emotional compared to Giovanni's powerful baritone. "But Serena… you have to trust us. We have to move quickly. Plan B is very time-sensitive. There isn't time to explain at the moment, but I promise we're not going to send you into the lion's den unarmed, so to speak. You're going to be okay. Just come with us."

Finally, I give in. There's no point in fighting it. What other choice do I have? Once again, I'm just a grieving pregnant woman with nowhere to go and no one to go to. My heart aches and my head is pounding. Not long ago, my life revolved around the Bathing Beauty and trying to help my mom through her sorrow.

How long has it been since I spoke with her? Not long, I remind myself. The party was only last night. But so much has happened since. I wish I could just return home, curl up in her lap, and lament my heartbreak. I think about how she was when she lost dad, and I almost start crying all over again.

But that's a luxury for later. I'll tell her where I am once I know it's safe. Until then, it'd be more dangerous for her—for anyone—to know where I am.

Giovanni and Orsina are offering a lifeline, whatever it may entail, and it would be stupid of me not to take it. So I follow them down the trail, listening to the insects chirping, the underbrush shaking with small animals just out of sight. Being surrounded by nature like this takes me back to those glorious, lazy days in the cabin with Luca, just the two of us with no distractions. Just loving each other in the calm woods, the outside world a distant memory.

It was all just a fantasy we'd concocted, though. We were hiding from the harsh reality, from the fact that he was a fugitive, from the fact that there were dangerous men hunting us down and wanting us dead.

I'd give anything to live that fantasy with him again, though.

With every thought of Luca, I can feel my heart breaking just a little more. But I can't help it. As much as it hurts me, I can't stop thinking about him. About how we were together. A perfect fit. I thought it was fate. Destiny. We overcame obstacles I never would have imagined possible. We've been through hell together, and we were finally on our way to the good part, the safe part.

Or so I thought.

I couldn't have been more wrong.

Who would have guessed it? Who could have ever seen this coming? Certainly not me. I was blinded by love, and I never expected the world to be so cruel as to snatch Luca away from me again. It's not fair. It's not right. We were supposed to be together forever, and we would have been. I know it. We were meant to be. I'll never love anyone the way I loved him. The way I *still* love him, and always will.

I'm so lost in my bittersweet memories that I zone out completely until we come to a stop suddenly, walking out of the shady woods and into a broad clearing. The sharp glare of sunlight on metal blinds me for a moment and I shade my eyes with my hand, blinking. There's a flurry of quick activity around me: Orsina taking my hand and pulling me toward the source of metallic light, Giovanni breaking away to speak in rapid Italian with another man, who is speaking Italian, too. I can only catch a word every now and then.

Biglietto.

Volo.

Prezzo.

And then Giovanni is helping me up a staircase. And my vision stops swimming, becomes clear and sharp. I finally realize what is happening. But by now, it's too late. I turn around, trying to run back down the stairs, but Giovanni is right behind me, keeping me there, stopping me from getting back down. My heart pounds, panic taking over my muddled mind.

"No! What are you doing? I'm not going! You can't do this!" I scream, slapping at Giovanni, trying to push past him. But he's like a brick wall. I glance down at the pavement below and see Orsina looking up at me with a pained expression.

"Orsina! Don't let them take me! I can't—I won't go!" I cry out. She shakes her head and looks away, refusing to get involved. All the while, Giovanni is marching me backwards up the boarding ramp toward the open door of the jet plane.

"Calm down, calm down," he's telling me. "It's going to be okay. Serena! You're going somewhere safe, somewhere they can't get to you."

Tears course down my cheeks.

"I don't want to go—I can't leave. What if—what if Luca needs me? I can't leave him here."

I know I'm not making sense, but I can't stop crying. Being in a different state from everything I ever knew was one thing. Getting on a plane and flying to who knows where?

I can't. I can't leave. I can't be so far away from him.

Giovanni pulls me into his arms in a hug suddenly, and after a moment I stop struggling, my tears dampening the front of his black shirt.

"Serena, he's gone. Luca's gone. But he's with you —okay? He's with you, wherever you go. You're not abandoning him. He's in your heart. And he would want you—and the baby—to be safe. Do you understand me?"

I break away and look into his face, but my vision is completely obscured by thick, crocodile tears.

"Listen to me," he says more quietly. "You're stronger than you think you are. Luca knew it. I know it. Deep down, you know it, too. I need you to find that strength, *si*? Find that strength and use it to take care of yourself and the baby. We're going to do everything we can to help you, but we can only help if you're willing. Got it?"

I give him a nod.

"Okay," I manage to choke out between sobs.

Giovanni pushes the hair back from my face, pats me on both shoulders, and then gives me a brotherly kiss on the forehead. "Don't worry. You're going to get through this, I know it. And someday, I'm sure I'll see you again, Serena. Hopefully under better circumstances."

Over my shoulder, he tells the flight attendant, "Take good care of her. She's one of our own. And keep a barf bag nearby. She's pregnant."

Then Giovanni turns me around and walks me through the opening to the jet. A flight attendant with a sweet smile takes my arm and leads me down the aisle to a comfortable, massive sofa-like seat complete with fluffy pillows and a downy blanket. As I settle into the seat, still totally in shock but knowing there's no point in struggling now, I turn back to see Giovanni. He gives me a wave, a hopeful smile that doesn't quite reach his eyes, and then he disappears. The door closes, and I'm alone in this plane.

Completely alone, in fact, except for the flight attendant. I'm the only passenger in this private jet, and I get the feeling this is not going to follow the usual prescribed route... wherever it is I'm going. As the plane starts to shake and rumble with lift-off, the flight attendant comes by and gives me two items—a barf bag, and a backpack. I set the first one aside and start to idly go through the contents of the back-pack. I pull out several printed tickets, a passport that looks exactly like the one I have at home, and a huge wad of cash—in euros.

No. No way.

I pick up one of the tickets with trembling hands.

The destination… Napoli, Italia.

"Holy shit," I murmur, and immediately reach for the barf bag.

I stare out the window of the airplane, my eyes glazing over as I watch the gray and lavender clouds drift lazily by. The moon just barely strains through, its light splintering through the sky while the dull hum and buzz of the engine almost lulls me to sleep. But I can't sleep. I've never been able to sleep on planes, even when I was little.

Of course, back then it was because I was too excited, too interested in gazing out the window and being in awe of how far up we were to feel sleepy at all.

My mom would fall asleep instantly, a silky pink eye mask over her face, her perfectly-lipsticked mouth hanging open and snoring. It made me laugh to see her looking like that, all undignified, especially since she was usually so prim and proper. My dad, on the other hand, would stay awake with me, playing card games or twenty-questions. We would make believe that we were the co-pilots of the plane, pretending we were soaring to some distant land like Malaysia.

I'm sure he would have liked to catch up on sleep like my mother did, but he never gave in. He always did his best to entertain me on long flights, and it made all the difference. Playing with him was a great distraction from my motion sickness, my nervousness at being stuck on a plane with a bunch of strangers. I never properly thanked him for doing all that.

I miss him. And I miss Luca.

Why do all the men I love have to leave me behind?

I turn around in the seat and look around the interior of the cabin. I've flown first-class before, of course, but I've never had a private flight. Being the only passenger on the plane is awkward. I feel like the stewardess has got to be watching me, wondering who the hell I am and why the hell I deserve such special treatment. And she would be right to wonder about that. After all, I'm nothing special, myself. I'm just a random pregnant lady to them, some stranger.

I can't help thinking that the only thing that made me special was the fact that Luca loved me. And now that he's gone? Well, who the hell *am* I?

I close my eyes and set my hands on my stomach,

trying to send reassuring thoughts to the little baby inside, even though I can hardly reassure myself. I remember reading that the stress a mother feels during pregnancy can affect the child.

That worries me, and that worry stresses me out even more.

I mean, even under normal circumstances, being pregnant is rough. I thought it would be a breeze with Luca at my side, but now everything has changed. I'm a single mom now, and I don't even have my own mom around to help me.

If I tell her where I am, then the mob will go after her. Force her to tell them everything. I can't put her in danger like that. I have to figure everything out on my own. I have to be strong for myself. I have to do it all.

But all I want to do right now is cry. I curl up in the seat as best I can, tucking my legs underneath myself, trying to get comfortable. But nothing feels right, and why should it? My whole world has been dumped upside down. Nothing makes sense anymore. I just wish somebody could tell me what to do, how to feel. My brain keeps circling back to Luca, those last beautiful moments we had together before he was ripped away.

His smile. His twinkling green eyes. The feeling of his hand holding mine.

My hands feel so empty and useless without his.

Despite how hard I've tried to fight it, the tears

start to fall again. My heart is broken, and it's impossible to imagine a time when that won't be the case. I know I'll never love like that again. Luca was my everything. He still is, even if he's not around to see it.

Suddenly, there's a gentle hand on my elbow. I turn quickly to see the flight attendant kneeling beside me with a worried expression.

"Miss, are you alright?" she asks softly.

I hastily wipe my eyes with my sleeve and give her a nod.

"Yeah, yeah. I'm fine."

She tilts her head to one side, looking unconvinced. "Are you sure? Is there anything I can get you? Soda? A glass of wine?"

"Oh, I-I can't," I murmur, sniffling. "I'm pregnant."

And saying that out loud, for some reason, releases the floodgates. I start to sob uncontrollably, the stewardess's eyes going wide at the sight of my sudden meltdown.

"Oh no, Miss, I'm sorry. That man did say you were pregnant, didn't he? I totally forgot. It's just such a habit to offer guests alcohol, I didn't mean to—"

I reach out and take her hand despite myself. I know I probably look like a complete weirdo, totally off my head. But I don't care right now. I just need a hand to hold.

"No, no, it's not the pregnancy. It's—it's just that m-my fiancé just died and I'm trying to hold it together but I'm pregnant and he's never going to get to meet his own child and I'm going to be all alone raising this baby and I'm so scared," I ramble all at once, the words stumbling over each other in between sobs. The flight attendant's face has gone totally red and I can tell I am absolutely the most distressing customer she has had, maybe ever.

To her credit, she doesn't recoil from the emotional hurricane that I've become. She sits down in the seat beside me and squeezes my hand.

"Oh, I am so sorry. That's terrible. I can't even imagine how hard this must be," she says genuinely, shaking her head.

"I miss him so much already and I don't know when this is going to stop hurting so bad," I confess tearfully. She pats my hand, nodding supportively.

"It may take some time," she says sagely.

"How long?" I ask, fully aware that I'm asking her questions she doesn't have an answer to, but unable to stop the flow of crazy emotions pouring out of me.

"Oh, I don't know the answer to that. But I can tell you that you're stronger than you think you are, and you're going to be okay," she adds, emphasizing every word to drive the point home. "You and that baby are going to make it out alright. I just know it."

"Thank you," I mumble, suddenly feeling very tired.

"Could I get you something to drink? And some tissues? What would you like?"

"Do you have ginger ale?" I ask, rubbing my stomach. The nausea is coming back.

She stands up quickly, releasing my hand. "Of course! I'll be back in just a minute."

She rushes down the aisle and comes back with a box of tissues and a little bottle of ginger ale, which she pours into a glass with a bendy straw. She sets it on the fold-down table in front of me and then asks, "Is there anything else I can do? Should I turn the lights down so you can relax a little better? You've got a long flight ahead of you. It might do you some good to try and sleep if you can manage it."

I take a sip of the ginger ale and try to fight down the urge to race to the bathroom and vomit. I'm finally just starting to feel comfortable and sleepy in my seat and the last thing I need is to get back up. I look up at the stewardess and say, "Okay. Yes. That would be nice. Thank you."

She brings me a bigger blanket and then turns down the lights, leaving me alone with my thoughts once again. I glance out the window to see the darkness settling in, the sky turning from light purple to dense navy blue. Every now and then I catch a glimpse of the moon, thin and hook-shaped between dark clouds. I force myself to close my eyes and try to relax, pushing every dark thought out of my mind. If I alone am responsible for this baby, then it's our best interest for me to get some sleep. Especially since I have no idea what awaits us when this plane lands.

Finally, slowly, I drift off to dream.

"Dolcezza! Could you get the camera?"

I come down the stairs with a pink diaper bag and a camera slung over my shoulder, walking into the nursery to see Luca looking amused and impressed. He's holding the baby in his lap, both dad and child staring at each other with lovely green eyes. Our daughter is barely old enough to hold her head up on her own and she's already trying to stand, pushing off Luca's lap with her pudgy little legs. On the crown of her head little curly sprigs of dark hair grow, and her cheeks are chubby and pink. She's giving her father a gummy, adoring smile.

"She's going to be an athlete. I just know it," Luca says. "Look at this!"

"I know," I tell him, shaking my head in awe at our little bad ass. "The other day in the living room I looked away for one second and when I looked back she was rolling over onto her stomach. I didn't even know that was possible at her age."

"I wish I'd been there for that," he says. "Did you get a picture of it?"

"Yeah, yeah, of course," I laugh. "Speaking of which..."

I flash a photo of Luca and the baby, her tiny legs struggling to straighten out and balance on his thighs. She blinks in surprise at the sound of the camera shutter, then giggles.

Luca chuckles. "She's perfect, you know that, right? A perfect kid."

"I'm sure we'll take it back once she gets to the terrible twos but... right now I totally agree with you on that," I answer, unable to stop grinning. Everything is going so well. The doctor yesterday at our checkup appointment said the baby is progressing even better than we hoped. She was born a few weeks earlier than we intended, so there had been some concern at first. But now she's blown all our expectations out of the water. She's got her father's strength, that's for sure.

She yawns and lets out a whimper. "Oh! Probably time for a nap, is it?" Luca coos, wrapping her in his arms with her little head on his shoulder. He stands up and walks over to the crib to gently lay her down. For a minute, she fusses, her sweet little face screwing up and turning pink like she might cry. But instead, she just yawns again and stretches out, her hands curling into tiny fists as she closes her eyes.

"What a good girl," Luca says, beaming down at her. I stand next to him watching our daughter fall asleep. My husband, my rock, my guardian angel, puts his arm around my shoulders and pulls me close. He kisses me on the cheek.

I turn to kiss him on the lips softly, then gaze into those glorious green eyes I adore so much. I smile. "I don't think I've ever been this happy," I whisper.

"Life just gets better and better," he murmurs back.

Thump.

"Luca!" I mumble, blearily opening my eyes.

I wake up with a sense of panic, the plane lurching to one side suddenly. It takes me a moment to find my bearings, looking around the cabin in confusion. The events of the past day or so come rushing back to me.

The explosion. The cars. The gunshots. The plane.

I look out the window to see the sun streaking through the clouds. It's morning. I've finally gotten some proper sleep. But now I'm forced to remember everything. Luca is gone. That dream… is only that. A dream.

Just then, my stomach turns and I hurriedly grab the backpack and get up from my seat, hobbling down the aisle to the bathroom to throw up. After I'm done, I look in the tiny square mirror and take note of the bags under my eyes, the paleness of my face. I look like the living dead.

I haven't eaten anything in a while and anything that might have still been in my system is certainly gone now. My stomach grumbles, as though it's agreeing with my assessment.

I wash my hands, splash some water on my face, and pull my hair back into a ponytail. Then I pull an oversized sweatshirt, sleek black leggings, and some comfy sandals out of the backpack and change into them, leaving my old clothes on the floor. I don't want them anymore. They just remind me of the last night Luca and I spent together, at that party, surrounded by people who cared about us.

My stomach growls again, taking me back to the present moment. I make the silent promise to myself that I'll find something to eat when the plane lands, whatever it takes.

When I come back out, the flight attendant gently informs me that we'll be landing in about half an hour. Nervousness overwhelms me instantly. It hits me that I don't know where exactly to go when we get there. I go back to my seat and start pulling more tickets out of the backpack Giovanni gave me. The first one is a ticket from Napoli to Taranto. A train ticket. I immediately feel sick again. I have never visited Naples before, but I've heard about how crowded and scary it can be for a not-so-savvy foreigner.

I must look green in the face because the stewardess comes back and says, "Sorry you're not feeling well. When I was pregnant with my son Tyler, I was the same way. Constantly sick. It got better around the fifth month, though. It'll get easier, I promise."

"I hope so," I tell her, forcing myself to smile weakly.

I spend the next thirty minutes clinging to the edge of my seat, closing my eyes and trying not to vomit again. I tell myself this is not the time for me to be fragile. I'm about to take on a solo journey in a foreign country. I don't speak Italian, even though my parents spoke it to each other occasionally when I was growing up. I dig through the backpack and find, to my relief, an English-to-Italian phrasebook. Paperwork, tickets, money, clothes, and now this? Apparently Giovanni thinks of everything.

I hardly have time to peruse the phrases, though, before the plane comes to a smooth landing. I gather up the backpack and its contents, get myself straightened out, and pool what little composure I have left. When I disembark, the flight attendant comes out with me. She takes me by the arm and gives me a confident smile.

"I'll help you with this next step, but then you're on your own, I'm afraid. But I have full faith in you. Napoli is busy and intimidating, but you can handle it," she says, walking me through the airport. We get to the busy street out front and my jaw drops. This place is packed with locals and tourists alike, everyone jabbering away in languages I don't understand. Lots of people give me death glares, dirty looks, scanning me up and down like they can tell instantly I'm not from around here. I feel very exposed, very vulnerable. Especially with my pregnant belly. Luckily, the oversized sweatshirt hides the teeny barely-there baby bump completely, but I still can't shake the feeling that people can just *tell* somehow.

The flight attendant hails a cab for me and helps me into the backseat with what little belongings I have, then turns to the driver and gives him instructions in Italian. The driver nods and looks back at me, saying, "I speak some English. I'm taking you to Napoli Centrale. *Si?*"

I nod, hoping that's correct. Just before the cab drives off, the flight attendant gives me a nod and a thumbs up. "Good luck!" she calls out as the window rolls back up.

It's about a fifteen-minute ride to the train station, and I spend nearly the whole time staring wide-eyed out the window at the bustling city passing by. Constant horn-honking, shouting, vendors racing after people going past their wares without looking. The cab driver weaves in and out of standstill traffic, only barely avoiding a collision over and over again. Finally, it starts to make me so nauseous that I give up and start perusing the backpack again, looking to see what else Giovanni left with me. To my infinite joy, I find a simple little cell phone, pre-programmed with all the necessary apps, a portable charger hooked up to it. This is a great discovery, since my American cell phone is long dead and I couldn't charge it overseas.

When we arrive at the train station, the cab driver helps me count out the euros to pay him, and then I get out and I'm alone again. Alone in this big, sprawling, teeming city full of strangers who don't speak the same language as me. I swallow back the bile creeping up my throat.

I need to be strong. For the baby. For Luca.

I hold my head up high and hoist the backpack over my shoulder, walking into the station as confidently as I can. Fake it 'til you make it, I remind myself. The girl that used to walk into a room, confident and wearing the season's hottest styles seems like a distant dream, but I try to conjure her up once more, even in the far less fashionable outfit I'm wearing now.

I check my ticket and find out which train to get on, looking up at a digital times-table hanging high in the lobby. Then I track down the proper platform and get there early, settling in on a bench to wait for my train. I keep my belongings close and my eyes peeled for potential pickpockets. If there's one thing I know about Naples, it's that you have to be careful. And so I am.

Now that the panic of figuring out where to go is over, I start focusing in on the people around me, the hurried conversations in Italian I can't understand. I feel so out of place without any real luggage and no one to travel with. Apart from taking the subway in the city back home, I don't usually take public transportation, and certainly not alone. I wish I knew what anyone was saying. It would feel much less isolating to know what was going on. I swear silently to myself that my baby will grow up speaking Italian and English if I have to hire someone to teach her.

Just as I'm getting lost in these thoughts, there's a commotion down the platform and I idly look over to see a big, burly guy arguing with a much smaller woman. She's gesticulating wildly, shouting in his face even as he towers over her with his hands balled into fists. It looks bad. Very bad. Like any second, true violence is going to erupt.

The train rolls up to the platform and I stand up to join the crowds ready to flood the train cars as soon as the doors open. But then I hear a scream and look over to see the big guy grabbing the young woman by her ponytail. I notice then that she has a baby bump that is much bigger than mine. And suddenly all I see is red.

Almost as though I have no control over my body, I start marching over to them, with no clue what the hell I'm going to do when I get there. By instinct, I catch a glimpse of an abandoned, broken umbrella lying under a bench. I snatch it up and walk up to the couple just as the big guy is winding his arm back to hit her in the face. My heart pounding so loud I can hear it in my ears, I swing the umbrella at full force, cracking the metal rod across the back of the guy's head.

He lets out a bellow of pain and surprise and

reflexively lets go of the pregnant girl. In an instant, I grab hold of her arm and yell, "Come on!"

The guy regains his sense and yells something most definitely vulgar in Italian and comes after us, but the girl and I manage to leap through the doors of the train just before they close. Shoving past confused, irritated passengers, I tug the girl along behind me through the train cars, trying to put as much distance between us and the doors as possible just in case her assailant managed to get in after us. But then I look to my left, out the window, and notice that the train is moving, leaving the station, and the big guy is still left on the platform. He's running after the train like an idiot, shaking his fist and swearing.

But we're safe inside, and I turn to the girl. She's pale and shaken, her eyes round and huge as she mutters breathlessly, "*Accidenti*, lady!"

My calm gaze rests on the Van Gogh painting hanging over the fireplace in my office as I listen to the soft sound of a pathetic excuse for a man sobbing in a chair behind me.

The painting is of a coastline, seen from the land, the perspective slightly raised up, as if the painter was standing on a hill. A small ship with a single rolled-up sail bobs in the water in the painting, and closer to the shore, a loose group of seven or so people stagger toward the sandy shoreline out of the water. Their faces are just blotches of color. The sky behind them is cloudy and gray, but there is light shining from behind the viewer, as if the shore is sunny.

Behind me, the man—as much as my mouth curls into a frown to call him that—blubbers a few words at me.

"Don Abruzzi, I...I don't know what I can say. My son, he's a good boy, he really is. He just lost his temper. He's young, he's hot-blooded, they're all like that."

"Your boy was rash," I say calmly, my gaze not moving from the painting on the wall. I'm seated still as a statue in my grand leather chair. "He picked a fight with one of my soldiers."

"He didn't know, Don Abruzzi," the man says, exasperated. "And he paid for it. Your man knocked out some of his teeth, he-"

"He's lucky he wasn't killed," I say matter-of-factly, slowly rising to my feet and folding my hands as I turn to look at him. The man is thin and middle-aged with graying hair, his eyes rimmed with red.

What a pathetic husk of a man.

"He understands that," the man says, nodding his head quickly. "Please, Don Abruzzi, I will take responsibility for anything we owe you because of this."

"I know you will," I say. "My soldier your boy fought with says it was over your daughter. I expect you'll tell her to show a little more respect to my men as well."

"Of course, I-"

"Moreover," I interrupt him, gesturing for one of the guards in the room to pour me a glass of wine, "Since it seems your boy has enough money to piss away in the bars picking fights with dangerous men,

I expect you can manage a fifty-percent increase in your monthly payments."

His eyes go wide, and his face goes pale. "What? Don Abruzzi, please, I've just sold my car to make my back-payments already, and-"

"Your protection is clearly more expensive than we realized," I continue, unfazed. "If your boy is so liable to get into trouble, it's only fair to charge more."

"Don Abruzzi, I won't be able to stay in business if-"

I stop listening to the man's squawling, and I glance to one of my guards. With the slightest nod of my head, two of them move toward the man and haul him to his feet. He continues to make any excuse he can come up with as my men drag him out of my office.

I glance at them going while I take a drink of the black wine offered to me.

Pathetic.

As he's dragged out, my consigliere passes him on the way into my office. He takes his hat off to me out of respect, and I give him a nod to allow him inside.

"Come in, Enrico."

Enrico enters, and my guards close the doors behind him while I invite him to have a seat and have them pour him some wine to join me.

"Him again?" Enrico asks with a wry smile,

nodding back to the door where I can still faintly hear the man crying out pleas for mercy. "You're a more patient man than me, Don Abruzzi."

I give a soft smile, then look back up to my painting.

"You see the people in this painting, Enrico? Every time I deal with men like that blubbering idiot, I look at this painting. Lost, weary parasites staggering into our territory, wanting just a taste of all the riches we've built up for ourselves here in New York. You give them just a taste, and they want more and more until they've drained you of every-thing. Push them too far, and they turn violent. It's all about knowing their breaking point—then you can keep them just where you want them. It's only fair."

"I'll drink to that," Enrico says with a broad smile, getting comfortable in his mahogany chair in what looks like a brand-new Armani suit.

We raise our wine glasses to one another. "*Salute,*" I toast before we take a drink and I sit back down behind my desk to face him. "Enough pleas-antries, though. Tell me, have you found what I've asked for?"

Enrico takes a moment longer than usual to enjoy the taste of his wine, and I have my answer before he's even spoken.

"We haven't been able to find the De Laurentis girl, no."

"Is she still in New York?"

"We should assume 'no.' Lomaglio still has close allies in the Costas, and they got her away from the car bomb fast."

Now it's my turn to give him an even, silent stare before I speak again. "You don't sound optimistic about it, Enrico. Care to share your thoughts?"

Enrico clenches his jaw a moment, and I can feel his nervousness like a stink on him.

"The Lomaglio guy...Luca. He isn't-"

"Wasn't," I correct him.

"*Wasn't* like the other Costas. He commanded their respect in a way the other capos can't. That kind of loyalty extended to Serena De Laurentis. Luca's friends are going to make sure she's far out of the way. They'll know it's no use stashing her in some safehouse around town."

"And you don't know how far they've taken her...why, exactly?"

"Her trail just vanishes, Don Abruzzi. Whoever got her away from the hit on Luca did it fast and quiet, and nobody's talking. We don't have the means to-"

"*Find* the means, Enrico," I say, letting the slightest impatient edge come to my voice. A calm demeanor means that it only takes a light touch to get my point across, when I want something done. I look him dead in the eye, my gaze steely. "I'm giving you freedom to use whatever funds necessary, and I want you to hire a professional to get this done. I want the De Laurentis line to end with that girl, and I want it to end sooner rather than later."

"I understand, Don Abruzzi," he says, bowing his head, but he hesitates a moment. "Finding someone for this job might be...costly. There is one more thing we've picked up on."

I raise an eyebrow at him.

"There are rumors going around about an announcement she made before the hit. Serena De Laurentis might be pregnant."

I don't let any reaction cross my features. Inside, I feel frustration brewing up like a storm. Every day either Serena De Laurentis or Luca Lomaglio is alive, it's an insult to the Abruzzi name. It's a testament to my own son's murder and a challenge to my authority. But some bastard spawn of the two of them...?

"Very well then," I say candidly. "Whoever you find can deal with the problem before she gives birth and it becomes two problems."

Enrico stares at me a moment, and the look in his eyes makes me tempted to replace him. He still clings to useless, outdated values that do nothing but cripple you in this city. I set my wine glass down and fold my hands.

"Enrico, my friend," I speak to him with the kindliness of a grandfather. "I shouldn't have to remind you how this works, you know. Luca Lomaglio is dead. We killed him. If the De Laurentis girl has a child, and that child is allowed to grow up, that's one more rival, one more person who will grow up bloodthirsty for *vendetta* against us, against everything we've built."

Enrico shifts ever so slightly in his chair, but he nods. I lean forward.

"Blood for blood. This is for Lorenzo, don't forget that. And if this 'pregnancy' thing is a rumor, then let's keep it as a rumor, nothing more. Do you understand me?"

"Of course, Don Abruzzi," Enrico says, apparently finding his manhood again and acting with some dignity. "It will be done."

"Good," I say, and I gesture for my guards to open the door as Enrico begins to stand up. "See to it. And while we're on the subject of rumors…"

"Right, about Luca," Enrico says as he stands up and I open my desk, taking out a small envelope. "Some of the men have been talking about how the hit went down. The soldiers talk—it's what they do. Nothing to be worried about."

"I know they talk," I say as I open the envelope and take out its contents. "Talk isn't good for business. Which is why I have these," I say, sliding a few photographs across the table. Enrico steps forward and looks at them, his eyes widening as he picks them up.

They show a large, burly, musclebound body

lying on fire-scorched asphalt...and a bloody stump where its head should be.

"This is all that remains of Luca Lomaglio," I say evenly, giving him a meaningful look as he glances up at me.

He opens his mouth to say something, but I talk again before he can. "Make sure these circulate among the men. Understood?"

He takes the envelope and sticks the photos back into it, swallowing hard. "Yes, Don Abruzzi."

I smile.

"Good man. Now go."

I watch my consigliere stalk off, and I gesture for my guards to go too, which they do, silently—the way I like it. The door finally closes behind them, leaving me in peace.

I let out a breath, feeling tired already. If I still had my youth, I'd be out taking care of this myself.

My eyes drift back to the painting on the wall as I finish off my wine in a single swig. I look at the face-less figures staggering onto the shore, and I know that not long ago, we were those people. *Cleaners*, they called us. It's only thanks to me that we can one day be called the Abruzzi Family and command the respect we deserve. And I'm not about to let some bitch and her unborn brat ruin our war for the Bronx for me.

Not her, not the Costas...

And certainly not the fact that I never was presented with Luca Lomaglio's corpse.

"*Grazie per l'aiuto*," says the girl softly. She's sitting across from me in the train car, the two of us having settled down into some seats with a table in between. She looks understandably nervous, picking at her pinkie nail and biting her lip as she looks up at me through thick eyelashes.

This girl doesn't look a day over twenty and my heart immediately goes out to her, my maternal or maybe sisterly instincts kicking in. I've never had a sister, as I grew up an only child, but already I feel like I want to rescue and protect this complete stranger. I have this urge to go back to that Napoli train platform and beat her assailant mercilessly with that umbrella I picked up.

I don't know where this aggressive mama-bear instinct is coming from. Maybe it's just the pregnancy hormones. Either way, I know I can't abandon this young lady now, even if I can't understand a word she's saying to me.

"*Non dovevi farlo,*" she adds emphatically, looking at me with mingled fear and gratitude. I realize suddenly how crazy I must look to her—a random woman who swept in to help her and is now sitting in front of her totally silent. My face starts to burn pink and I give her a smile.

"I-I'm sorry, I don't speak Italian," I tell her quietly, glancing around. Nobody else in the train seems even slightly interested in us, which is a relief. Everybody is staring down at their books or iPads or phones, earbuds in, totally in their own little worlds. I start to let my guard down just a little bit. At least for now we should be relatively safe.

Meanwhile, the girl across from me has lit up, a big smile brightening up her pretty but solemn face. She looks completely different when she smiles, I notice. She leans forward as though to tell me a secret or something and says, "You speak English? I speak English!"

"Oh," I reply, surprised. "Well then, hi. Nice to meet you! I'm Serena—Serena Smith," I tell her, only barely stopping myself from giving her my real last name. I know I'm probably being way overly cautious, but after the events of the past couple days, I'm not feeling particularly safe sharing details with anyone, even someone who seems so vulnerable and innocent as this girl.

She giggles and holds out her hand for me to shake. "My name is Francesca Valenti," she introduces herself. "Are you American?" she asks, barely able to hide her curiosity.

I laugh. "Yeah, what gave me away? The accent?"

Francesca nods, sitting back against the seat. She looks more relaxed now, and I'm starting to calm down a little bit myself. "What brings you to Napoli?" she asks.

"Just doing some traveling," I lie quickly, but then when I remember I don't have any luggage with me and I don't have a backstory all plotted out in my head, I correct myself. "Actually, if I'm being honest, I-I'm kind of running away from… something."

Francesca's dark brown eyes go wide. She leans forward again, glancing around before whispering, "Like… the police? Did you rob a bank or something?"

I snort and shake my head. "Oh god, no. Nothing like that. I'm not a criminal," I assure her, although when I consider my association with the Costa crime family, I think I might actually qualify as a criminal myself. Or at least an accomplice. And with the cops in the Cleaner's pocket, is that really even a distinction for them? "Just had some kind of bad stuff happen recently back home and I needed to get away for a while. Clear my head. Start over, maybe."

As I'm saying all this out loud, it's almost more like I'm telling myself than Francesca. It's hitting me just how little I know about what the future holds for me. My stomach turns and I have to sit very still and focus on not getting sick again. I close my eyes for a second and grit my teeth. When I open my eyes again, Francesca's face looks solemn and sad again.

"You are pregnant, too," she says, her voice barely above a whisper.

"How'd you guess?" I ask, frowning. I'm not really showing yet, my stomach still relatively flat unless you're looking really hard.

"You just turned green as pea soup," she replies, shrugging. "I know the look. I feel the same way. It's strange—people call it 'morning sickness' but I've been feeling sick all day, not just in the morning. Is it the same for you?"

I give her a nod. Of course, I still don't quite know if my nausea is due to pregnancy or just a side effect of all the horrible events that have happened to me lately, but I'll go ahead and blame it on the pregnancy. Might as well. It's easier to think about being pregnant than it is to think about losing Luca and the life I thought I was going to lead.

"Your husband… is he meeting you in Taranto?" Francesca inquires, gently patting her pregnant belly as she glances at the engagement ring on my finger. I have to bite my lip and clench my fists under the table to keep from crying. Oh, how I wish that were the truth. If only Luca would be waiting for me on the platform when I arrive down south. If only I could end this day in his arms, happy and safe at last.

But that's just not my reality anymore, and there's no point in pretending it still is.

"No," I answer, staring down at the polished-wood table between us. "He's… not with me anymore. He's gone."

"He left you? While you're pregnant?" she retorts, looking downright scandalized. "Men!"

I have to smile a little bit, despite the ache in my heart. If only that were the problem here.

"No, he didn't leave me by choice," I explain slowly. "I… lost him."

It takes a moment for Francesca to catch my meaning. Her frown gradually softens into an expression of extreme pity, and that look on her face almost breaks my heart for the thousandth time. She reaches across the table to place her hands on my forearm, looking terribly sad.

"Oh no. I am so sorry," she says, those big brown eyes going shiny with tears. "I can't imagine how you must feel. You poor thing."

I take her hands in mine and give them a squeeze. It was so weird, having a woman so much younger than me, someone I just saved from an abusive man, become so maternal to me in turn. But it feels nice to have someone show me some softness. The past couple days have been so sharp, so painful, that it's almost a relief to not have to be strong right now. I can just be honest, even if I can't tell her every detail.

"I'll be okay. I think," I assure her, hoping desperately that I'm right about that.

"You will be," she says, nodding vigorously. "You can handle it. Look at you, traveling all by yourself in a foreign country. You will be okay."

I smile even as I can feel my eyes burning with tears. Somehow, hearing this young girl say it, I can almost believe that it's true. That I *will* be alright. But I don't want to think about it much more right now. We've got a long ride ahead of us, and I need a distraction. So I decide to turn the spotlight back on Francesca. After all, I'm obviously not the only one here with a tragic backstory.

"Enough about me," I say, "what about you? Who was that guy messing with you on the platform? And was I right to step in and intervene? I didn't even think about it—I just did it."

Francesca tosses her thick, golden-brown curls over her shoulder and her pretty face turns sour at the mention of the guy on the platform. She crosses her arms over her chest, narrowing her eyes. "That was the father of this baby, if you can believe it."

"What happened?" I push on, leaning forward to show my interest. And I am truly interested—I need to think about someone else's story for a change.

"He's a big, stinking *stronzo* is what happened," she proclaims. "That bastard has ruined my life for too long. He wasn't like that at first, you know. We went to school together, Pietro and me. We have known each other since we were very small. He used to pull my hair when he sat behind me in class, but everyone said he only did it because he liked me. Of course, my mama said to watch out for him, that he doesn't respect his mother and so he cannot be expected to respect me either, but I was stupid. And in love. I trusted him, you know? I thought he could be the one. Childhood friends! Everybody said we were so cute together. We've been dating since we were fourteen years old. I thought we were going to be together forever and everything would be perfect. How could it go wrong, you know?"

Her cheeks flush red and I can see that she's on the verge of tears. I give her a sympathetic look and shake my head. "It sounds so perfect, doesn't it?"

"*Si!* Exactly! I had no idea he would turn out to be so… so… *orrendo*. For a few years, it was all okay. He went out too much, he stayed out too late. He talked to other girls, sometimes right in front of me, just to cause a scene and make me cry. But he never laid a hand on me. I told myself that as long as the worst he did was make me jealous, I could deal with it. Some people have it so much worse, you know? That's what I told myself. He never laid a hand on me until about a year ago. And it came out of nowhere. One night I was cooking dinner and he came home from work looking so angry. I asked him what was wrong and he yelled at me, said he got fired and now he had to come home and be interrogated by his own girlfriend. I wasn't interrogating him, though. I just asked him what was wrong. I thought maybe I could make him feel better. But then he hit me. Just slapped me right across my face," Francesca says tearfully, pointing to her left cheek. She sniffles.

"Oh my god," I breathe, shaking my head angrily. "I can't believe he did that."

"It was bad," she agrees, wiping her eyes. "That was only the first time, and I thought it was only going to be the one time. I thought it would never happen again. But he never apologized, and it only got worse from that day on. He couldn't find a new job and every day he gave up a little more and a little more until finally he just stopped even looking for work. He just stayed home all day while I went to work. I am—*was*—a waitress at a cafe in our neighborhood. At night, he would go out with his friends to drink and party. And then he would come home after midnight and wake me up. He was always angry when he came home. Sometimes he would just go to sleep on the sofa. But other times he would get me out of bed and pick a fight with me. I was so tired, working all the time, but he would drag me out of bed and hit me."

"Francesca, that's horrible," I tell her, my heart racing with fury. I feel like this girl is my sister, my responsibility. Like I need to protect her. Hunt down that awful man and make him pay.

She nods, clearly struggling to regain her composure. I can relate. It's hard to keep all that pain tucked away. It's always trying to break free, burst through and break your heart again.

"And then," she adds, lowering her voice, "five months ago, I found out I was pregnant. I don't know how it happened. I was so careful. I've always wanted a baby, but I knew it wasn't safe to have a family with Pietro. If he hurt me so badly and I am a grown woman, how much damage could he do to a little child? I couldn't put them through it."

"Of course. That makes sense," I assure her.

She continues. "I had to hide it from him. And I wanted to escape, but I couldn't just leave. I know it sounds crazy, but I still loved him, and I kept thinking if he could just find a job and feel like a man again, he would stop hurting me. I've been with Pietro for six years. I didn't want to give up on our dream. I still thought maybe he would come around, that I had nine months to figure it out and make him love me again."

"How did you keep it a secret from him?" I ask her, confused. She stares down at the table, looking sorrowful again. Then she looks back up at me and shrugs.

"He just thought I was getting fat. He called me names, made fun of me for gaining weight. He even tried to make me skip meals, saying he wouldn't be caught dead with a fat girlfriend."

"What an asshole!" I burst out.

"It didn't even cross his mind that I might be pregnant, and I didn't want him to know, so I just let him think I was gaining weight instead. The insults were still better than him finding out I was pregnant," she reasons. "I thought once he started working again, he would stop mistreating me, and then I could come clean and tell him. So at first, I just looked around, trying to find work for him in secret. I asked everyone I knew. I tried everything. But whenever I suggested anything, whenever I told him there was a job opening, he would only get angry with me. He said I was just like his mother, bothering him instead of treating him like a man."

"That's not fair," I tell her. She nods.

"I know. I was only trying to help. But the longer he was out of work, the worse he got. I began to realize that there was no hope for us. No hope for the baby if I stayed with him. It was time to move on, to escape with my child before Pietro could find out I was pregnant. So I started hiding money from him. I was building a little escape fund so I could buy a ticket and leave. I was going to start over somewhere else, find a place to live and a new job and support the baby all on my own. I don't know anyone who has done that. But for me, it seemed like the only option. Finally, I saved up enough money to get out.

I was going to buy train tickets and put a deposit on an apartment in Salerno, get a museum job. I was all ready to go," she says.

"What happened?" I ask.

"Well, about a month ago when I came home from work, Pietro was still at home," she says, taking a deep breath. "I was surprised to see him there, because he was usually out with his friends when I got off work. But he was there, and he was waiting for me. At first, I thought maybe he was going to apologize to me, stop his routine of spending all my money and disappearing during the night. But then I realized he was holding the little box where I was keeping my escape money. He found it. He found all of it."

"Oh no," I gasp, feeling sick.

"He was so mad at me. He screamed at me, called me horrible names. He said I was a snake, a lying whore, for keeping all that money away from him. He dumped it all on the floor and told me to pick it up and hand it back to him. I did what he told me to do, but then I begged him to please just let me take the money so I could leave. I asked him to please just let me go."

"What did he do?" I almost hesitate to ask.

Francesca sighs. "He spent it all. Everything I had in that box. He took it with him when he went out that night and spent every last euro. And when he came back in the morning, he kicked me out, made me go stay on a friend's couch. Even though I pay for the apartment. Of course, my friend was angry. She called Pietro on the phone and yelled at him for treating me so badly, but when she was scolding him she accidentally let it slip that I'm pregnant. She said *'Pietro, you're a bastard for mistreating the woman you love, especially when she's carrying your baby.'* And then it was out."

"What did he do?"

She rolls her eyes. "I don't think he even knew what to do. One minute, he would yell at me, saying he would never be a father to our child. The next minute, he would curse me for keeping it a secret from him. He told me to get the hell away from him, but then he said that if I ever tried to leave him, he would kill me. I didn't know where to go. I was so afraid to leave the house that I couldn't go to work. I lost my job. All my money went to paying for the apartment even though I wasn't living there anymore. Then, last night, he showed up at my friend's house. He screamed and banged on the door until I came out. He had a baseball bat. He said he was going to beat me until I wasn't pregnant anymore."

"Holy shit," I mutter.

"I was lucky. My friend called the police and they took him away for the night. But I knew I couldn't stay in town. Not anymore. So this morning my friend drove me to the train station and I bought a ticket to Taranto. I knew he probably wouldn't follow me there. He's a born-and-raised Napolitano. He wouldn't leave Napoli for me," she explains. "But somehow, he found out I was leaving. He showed up at the station. He bought a ticket to get through the security and followed me to the platform. He grabbed me, said whether I lived or died, it was all up to him. Not me. He said he was going to throw me in front of a train. That's where you came in."

"I had no idea it was that bad," I murmur, totally shaken.

Francesca nods, a sad smile crossing her face. "You saved me, Serena. I don't know what to do when I get to Taranto, but at least I'll be away from Pietro. I'll be alive. Because of you."

I reach across the table and take her hands. "I don't know what I'm going to do when we get there either, but I know one thing for sure—we'll do better if we stick together."

Her smile widens, her big brown eyes glittering. "Okay."

~

It's late afternoon when we arrive in Taranto, the two of us achy and exhausted from traveling while pregnant. When we step off the train into the tiny, dimly-lit station, a wave of panic seizes me. I realize that I have no clue where we are and no clue where to go.

"Have you ever been here before?" I ask Francesca.

She shrugs. "Once, when I was a kid. I don't remember much, though."

"Well, first things first: we need to find somewhere to stay for the night," I say.

Francesca nods. "*Si*. It's not safe to be out after dark. Not for… girls like us. But I don't have much money left. Pietro—he took my purse as soon as he found me."

I turn to her and take her hand. "Don't worry. I can pay."

She shakes her head, those curls bouncing around. "No, no. I couldn't possibly accept your money, Serena."

"Don't be silly. I'm not going to let you sleep in the street. We can find a hotel somewhere, get a room for a couple nights until we figure out what to do," I tell her firmly, not taking no for an answer. I've already kind of adopted her as my sister, my responsibility.

"Are you sure?" she asks, looking genuinely torn-up over the idea of my paying for her.

I smile. "Of course. We're in this together."

We walk out of the train station and immediately Francesca hails us a cab. We ask the driver to take us to a hotel, any hotel, and he drives us into the city center. We get out in front of a place that looks a little ritzy for our taste. I have money, but I don't know what lies ahead for me in the future. I don't know how long this money is supposed to last me. So we walk a couple streets over and find a hotel that looks considerably less fancy. We go inside and Francesca talks to the concierge desk clerk, booking us a room for the night.

The sun is sinking down over the horizon when we go up to our room, both of us dog-tired and overwhelmed. It's hitting me just how strange our predicament is—two young pregnant women in a foreign city, with no luggage and no plans. We order some food for delivery and settle down to eat, turning on the television to distract from how awkward and bleak our situation seems.

After dinner, Francesca says, "Ugh, I've got a craving for ice."

"Pregnancy craving?" I ask, lying back on one of the beds.

She nods. "I don't know why, but every time I eat now I want ice after."

I laugh. "I suppose there are worse cravings to have."

"That's true," she agrees. "I think there's an ice machine on the floor below us. I'm going to see if I can get some. I have some change in my pocket Pietro didn't find."

"Okay. Be careful," I tell her, feeling like a mother

hen. She smiles and heads out, wobbling just a little bit with her hands on her belly.

I hoist myself up from the bed, thinking of taking a shower before bed. I walk into the bathroom and turn on the water, but just before I start taking off my clothes, I hear a knock at the hotel room door. I frown, confused for a moment, and then I realize it's probably just Francesca having forgotten to grab her room key. I walk over to the door and open it.

Immediately, I'm shoved backward, someone bursting through the door and slapping a hand over my mouth before I can scream. He pushes me against the wall and shuts the door behind him, his eyes black and shiny in the dim light.

"Quiet," he hisses. "I don't hurt you. You Serena De Laurentis, *si?*" His English is broken, but I understand well enough.

I just barely nod, hoping that this guy isn't about to kill me.

"*Bene*. They send me to help. I am Costa *fratello*. We supposed to meet at train station, but you not alone. I follow and wait. Who is the other girl?" he asks gruffly.

He takes his hand off my mouth.

"That's just a girl I met on the train. She—she's in trouble. Like I am," I explain.

"We must go. Before she come back."

"No," I protest. "I'm not going to just leave her behind."

"Cannot trust her. Could be enemy *informatore*."

"Francesca? No. She's not an enemy. She's just a girl who needs help. I'm not going anywhere without her," I tell him emphatically.

"We go now. Quick."

"No!" I shout, and he cups his hand over my mouth again. I glare at him, balling my hands into fists. He searches my face with his eyes for a minute. Then he sighs.

"You trust her?"

I nod, still staring him down. The man groans and releases me. I back away from him and fall back onto the bed, my heart racing. He looks over at me. "When she come back, we go."

"Okay."

A few minutes later, Francesca comes back in carrying a little bucket of ice chips. She's humming to herself, a smile on her face—until she notices the man in the room with us. Her eyes go wide and she stops in place, like she's paralyzed at the sight of him.

"Who—who is this?" she asks softly.

The man looks her up and down, then gives me a nod. My shoulders slump, relief taking over. "He's here to help us, Francesca. He knows my... my people back home. He's going to take us somewhere safe."

"Are you sure?" she asks, looking at the man sidelong with suspicious eyes.

I get up and walk over to link my arm with hers. "Yes. We can trust him."

She turns to me and shrugs. "Okay. But I'm taking the ice with me."

I smile. The man leads us both out of the room, down the stairs, and into the lobby. We leave the room keys by the front desk and walk down the street. The man helps us into an old-fashioned, classic black car, and drives us off into the night.

I wake up to the sound of a rooster crowing, as I often do, just before dawn. I open my eyes, letting them slowly adjust to the near-darkness of the bunk room. Across the property, the rooster cries again, and I smile to myself. He's getting a little overly excited about his job as alarm clock for the women's shelter commune, but that's okay. We keep him around because the lady chickens like him, and the lady chickens give us eggs. Most of the eggs, we sell at the local weekly open-air market along with produce we grow and breads we bake, but we keep a good portion of the eggs we collect and the plants we grow for our own kitchen, as well.

It was nearly two months ago that the mysterious Costa contact showed up in my hotel room and whisked Francesca and I away to this place. At first, we were both overwhelmed, in shock at how drastically our lives changed in such a short amount of time.

Francesca, of course, fit in quickly. She speaks Italian fluently, and she's so young and bubbly that everyone adores her.

I, however, struggled to get by. In the space of several months, I've gone from a New Yorker with a bright future and my own business to an essentially homeless, friendless foreigner in a country I've never lived in before. The guy who brought us here assured me that he would get word to my mother back in the States, tell her that I'm okay and that she should not go looking for me under any circumstances. I'm sure that conversation, if it did indeed happen, was not a particularly enjoyable one. But whatever he told her must have been pretty convincing, because she hasn't shown up on our doorstep to take me back to New York yet.

And the more time that passes, the less I feel like an outsider here. At first, I was quiet. I was still grieving—and honestly, I still am—and without being able to speak Italian, there wasn't much by way of social interaction for me. I clung to Francesca for a couple of weeks. It's not that the other women here aren't friendly. They've been welcoming and kind to me since the start. But it wasn't until I started picking up Italian that I began to branch out and open up to them.

Francesca helped translate what I couldn't understand, and we made flash cards. She quizzed me on Italian and I taught her what I know about running a business. She says that once the baby is born and she gets back on her feet, she wants to open her own version of Bathing Beauty here. It will be difficult, but she's plucky and determined enough to do it, I think.

Nowadays, I can just about hold a fluent conversation with the other women here, and I've taken on some responsibilities on the property. I help with the cleaning and the cooking of meals. A few days a week I have garden duties, and on the other days I bake bread. There's a lot to do in order to keep this place running smoothly, and even though I'm pregnant, so are many of the others. We all help out and do our part. We support each other. We listen to each other's stories and lend a shoulder to cry on. I've always been kind of a loner, even when I was at the height of my high school popularity food chain. I just relied on myself, until I found Luca again, and then I relied on him.

But now? I am part of a community. The women here are my friends and family and coworkers all rolled into one. Sometimes it does feel crowded here. It's hard to find much time to myself, since we all share bedrooms and bathrooms and living spaces.

But honestly, it's probably for the best that I don't get much alone time. This place keeps me busy and distracted so I'm not constantly thinking about the horrific events which led me here. At night… that's when those thoughts creep back in. I toss and turn most nights, reliving the good moments I had with Luca as well as the bad—the day I lost him forever. And every day, my stomach gets a little tiny bit rounder, reminding me over and over again that Luca will never get to meet his own child.

I roll out of bed and stretch, turning on the lamp on the little table between my bed and Francesca's. She groans and squints in the light, turning onto her side and pulling the pillow over her face to block it out. I laugh and walk over, taking the pillow and tossing it aside. It's a routine we do almost every morning. The more pregnant she gets, the less of a morning person she is.

"How is it already morning?" she asks in Italian.

"Well, let's see: it was night, and now that's over, so it's morning," I reply, smirking.

She opens her eyes and gives me a look of mild annoyance. "Smart-ass," she says in English. I nudge her shoulder.

"Come on. Time to get up. Let's go feed the chickens," I tell her.

"Ugh," she moans, sitting up in bed and rubbing her eyes. "Why are you always so happy in the morning? It's too early to be happy."

"Staying busy keeps me sane," I answer with a shrug. "As long as I keep moving, my brain can't catch up to me and make me think of stuff I don't wanna think about."

"Makes sense," she says, yawning. "Still would rather stay in bed, though."

"I'll meet you in the courtyard in fifteen minutes," I tell her with a wink. Then I get up and head down the hallway to the big communal bathroom. I slip into one of the shower stalls and hang my clothes up over the door. There are already a couple of other women in here, singing and humming in the stalls. There's a lot of singing here.

I think we all like to keep our minds busy, and thinking about lyrics and melodies is just another way of keeping bad thoughts at bay. Everyone here has a sad story. Everyone here has seen hard times. In a way, it's kind of helpful to know I'm not alone. By comparison, some of them have been through way worse stuff than I have.

Still, it doesn't make the pain any less awful. I still think about Luca every day. Every hour of every day, actually. He's always there, in the back of my mind, and there's still a tiny part of me that hopes he will one day come strolling through the front entrance of the shelter to rescue me and make me his bride like we planned. I still dream of the day when we can miraculously be a family together. I know it's probably hurting me more, prolonging the pain, to think about stuff like that. But I can't help it. It's like my heart doesn't understand that he's gone and he isn't coming back. No matter how hard my brain tries to convince me, my heart just keeps on believing.

After my shower, I dry off and get dressed. Most of the clothes we wear here are hand-me-downs, donations from thrift shops and such. I don't mind. It's not like I'm trying to impress anybody these days. My jeans and oversized sweater are comfortable enough to get work done while wearing them, and that suits me just fine.

Sometimes it does get a little claustrophobic, though, just hanging around the commune all the time. Some of the other women get to go out, get part-time jobs, volunteer in the community. The best I can hope for is to go to the weekly open-air market and help run the vendor stand. It's nice to get out and see different things every now and then, so I'm grateful for that. I would love to go out and wander around town, do some exploring with Francesca at my side. Go to a restaurant and order in Italian, since I could actually do that now.

But the man who brought me here was very emphatic about the security risks involved with my residence here.

He made the woman who runs this place, Daniela Russo, swear that she would keep me under lock and key. And she has. I understand that it's all for my safety, but it's still hard to be cooped up here all the time.

Daniela has recently put me in charge of feeding

the chickens, even though I'm not allowed to touch them, collect the eggs, or clean the coops since I'm pregnant. Francesca helps me feed them, and a couple other women who aren't pregnant do the other parts.

My favorite part of the morning is now—when I walk out into the courtyard and all the chickens come running up to me because they associate me with food. I jokingly told Francesca once that it's nice to feel loved, even if it's only by a group of hungry birds. And it's true. Despite all the warmth and camaraderie I feel surrounded by the women here, I'm still starving for love. Specifically, Luca's love.

I keep wondering if maybe someday I'll stop searching for him in every shadow, listening for his voice in every silence. Somehow, I doubt it. I think my heart is going to keep looking for his heart for the rest of my life. And if I have to be content with that, I guess I'll make my peace.

I spend the day going about my usual chores. I clean our bedroom and help clean the bathroom. I make coffee and set out baked goods for breakfast. I help tend to the garden, pulling weeds and picking ripe heirloom tomatoes. In the afternoon, Francesca and I sit down to watch an Italian soap opera I've gotten embarrassingly addicted to, and after that we head to the kitchen to start working on dinner for everybody.

I'm boiling a massive pot of water on the stove when suddenly there's an ear-piercing scream from across the compound. My heart stops for a moment and I immediately turn off the stove and start running toward the sound, thinking that one of the older women has probably fallen and hurt herself.

But before I even make it out of the kitchen, someone pulls me into the pantry and shuts the door, putting a hand over my mouth.

It's a strangely familiar sensation, and I quickly realize that it's the man who brought me here six weeks ago. I stare at him wide-eyed and confused, wondering why the hell he would do this. I need to go see what's going on out there. I need to help my fallen friend.

I point toward the door, hinting that I need to leave, but the man shakes his head. Then I hear a few more screams, clearly from my fellow shelter women, and then *male* voices. They shout out in Italian, "Where is she? Where is Serena De Laurentis?"

My heart sinks.

"We will not hurt you. We have no interest in you. Bring Serena De Laurentis to us. Now."

My eyes well up with tears. How did this happen? How did they find me? How did the Cleaners come all the way from America to track me down here, in this most modest and unexpected of places?

Then I remember something slightly strange that happened last week at the open-air market. A young man with heavy, black brows came up. I cheerily explained our wares—tomatoes, zucchini, onions, garlic, peas, beans—but he wasn't interested. He simply stared at me, those black eyes boring into my face until finally I stopped talking. He disappeared into the crowd soon after, and I just chalked it up to a random weird occurrence. Maybe he thought he recognized me or something. Or maybe he was just an oddball.

But now it dawns on me that he probably did recognize me, and he had been hunting for me all this time, only to find me selling produce in the south of Italy with hardly a care in the world. I swallow hard. There's only one choice for me, isn't there? I certainly can't let the Cleaners hurt my friends here. No. I have to walk out of this pantry and hand myself over before anyone gets seriously injured. That's what I have to do. It's the right choice.

"Let me go," I manage to whisper behind the man's hand. He shakes his head again.

"No," he mouths at me. Then, still holding onto me, he edges toward the back of the pantry and scoots aside a barrel of canned goods to reveal a trap door in the floor. I stare at it in confusion. Has that really been here all this time? Just waiting for me in case I need to break away?

I guess I underestimated the severity of my situation. These Cleaners aren't like Pietro—they didn't give up on hunting me after I left town. They followed me here, like bloodhounds to a scent. And suddenly, it's like the past six weeks don't even matter. I was a ticking time bomb all along, a liability to all the wonderful women here who have become almost like family.

"You go. Downstairs. Find the door. Run the tunnel. Don't stop," the man explains in broken English, his voice scarcely audible. "Come to a field. Keep running. Find the villa. Old. Ruins. Hide there and wait."

"What about my friends?" I ask, my eyes filling with tears.

"I protect them," he says simply. And I know there's nothing I can do. I have to believe him. I have to believe that he can save them. Still, I hesitate.

"Worse for them if you stay," the man adds, sensing my reluctance.

I can feel another piece of my heart shattering. This is the way it has to be.

So without wasting another second, I climb down through the trap door, down a rickety ladder, and find myself standing behind a shelf of odds and ends. When I step out around the shelf, I realize I'm in a basement.

I knew about the basement, of course. It's where we keep old clothes, preserved produce, and other stuff we don't have a place for. I've been in here before, but never through a trap door in the ceiling. I look around, floundering in the low light as I run my hands up and down the grimy walls until I find a door handle. With my heart fluttering, I turn the handle and step through the door into a cold, dark tunnel. I take a deep breath, close the door behind me, and start running with only the light of my cell phone screen to guide me. I run nearly blind, tears blurring my vision as I try not to sob, my footsteps soft on the muddy ground. I keep running until my legs feel weak, until my chest feels tight. I walk for a little while to regain my breath, and then I start running again.

I don't know how long I'm underground, but when I finally come to a round wooden door and push it open to expose myself to the cool air, the sky is dark overhead. I climb out of the ground and close the hatch behind me, covering it with dirt before I keep going. Just as the man described, I'm in a field. It looks to be the middle of nowhere. I can't hear anything but the wind.

I force myself not to think about Francesca. I force myself not to think about Daniela and the other women I left behind, the new family I've already lost and possibly endangered. I trudge onward, my feet feeling heavy and my heart racing. My lungs hurt. I'm out of breath, feeling dizzy and weak. But I have to keep going. For all I know, the Cleaners are hot on my trail, and I have no idea what my next move is. Where the hell can I go? Where can I hide?

These guys will always find me, won't they?

I keep walking through the dark, my phone battery quickly draining. I turn it off to save battery power and just walk blindly in the night, hoping the Cleaners don't find me before I can reach the next checkpoint. After what feels like hours and hours of walking, the massive shape of a white building looms in front of me. I squint in the moonlight, trying to make sense of the shape I'm seeing. I take in pillars, piles of rubble. A marble archway.

My heart skips a beat. There it is. That has to be it. The old ruined villa.

I race forward, hurrying to climb over the broken-down walls and slip through a busted window, tearing my sweater on a piece of jagged glass, but feeling grateful it wasn't my skin that got slashed. I stumble into what looks to have once been a grand living room of some kind, and I all but collapse on the concrete beneath me, out of breath and overwhelmed.

As soon as I'm sitting down, my body aches with relief. I lean back against a marble column and try to catch my breath, closing my eyes as the tears trickle down my cheeks. And now that I'm still, it's like all those horrible thoughts catch up to me.

Is this the way it's always going to be?

Temporary lodging? Temporary friends?

The constant threat of being discovered and chased out of hiding, only to find another little hole in the ground to cower inside? Am I going to spend the rest of my life on the run? And what about when my baby is born? How the hell can I raise a child like this—always running from one place to the next with no stability, no safety, no place to call home?

Am I going to end up this way over and over again? Alone and afraid?

Luca's face swims to the front of my mind. Smiling at me as he knelt down to ask me to be his wife. I said yes. I said yes, but it doesn't matter because he's gone and he's never coming back and I'm never going to be anybody's wife.

I'm so damn tired. I need to sleep. My whole body is giving up. I pull my knees up inside the oversized sweater and lie down on my side, the cold concrete instantly giving my body hell. It's not comfortable, and it's almost certainly not safe, but that's just the way my life is going to be from now on. The sooner I get used to it, the easier it will be.

I hope.

So I lie here quietly, breathing in the dusty air of the crumbling old villa, slowly drifting off into the closest thing to sleep I can hope for. I don't know how much time passes, and I don't know if I ever actually fall asleep for real, but out of the darkness and the silence comes the unmistakable sound of footsteps echoing in my broken-down fortress. I sit up, sleepy and defeated, to await my assailant. Will he take me captive? Torture me? Kill me?

It doesn't matter anymore. Not really. In a way, I almost welcome it. I'm tired of being on the run. Maybe it's time to just face up to the monster, let fate do what it will with me.

A voice splits the silence, deep and questioning.

"Passerotta mia?"

This strong heart of mine has held up through beatings, gunfights I never thought I'd survive, and being baptized in fire. All the while, it's been steady, fierce, and unstoppable. It's a heart that refused to stop beating, all for the sake of Serena.

And the sight of my Serena shakes it like never before.

I rush forward to her, the love of my life, as her eyes go wider than I've ever seen them. I worry that she's about to pass out, so before she can even start to scramble to her feet, I stoop down and wrap my arms around her, cradling her as gently as the most precious treasure on the earth. On pure instinct, her arms go around the rippling muscles of my neck, and she melts into me, hot tears wetting my shoulders as her whole body shakes with her sobs.

We say nothing more to each other for what feels like an eternity. It's been so long, so painfully long since I've felt her touch, held her in my arms, enjoyed the very warmth of her body on my skin. I savor it, and I feel my own tear roll down my stony face as I breathe in the scent of her hair that I've missed so badly.

"Luca?" she manages through sobs at last, and the sound of her voice melts my heart.

I can hear so much pain in her.

"I'm here," my deep voice rumbles, holding back my own tears as I feel her body—delicate yet strong as steel all at once—trembling in my arms. My hand moves up to the back of her head, and I stroke her hair gently, kneeling down to sit down fully beside her.

It feels like we've been together for hours already, just riding out another of life's storms together, emotion flowing freely between us. I feel her heart beating against mine as I hold her, and I turn my face to kiss her on the head as her whole body shakes again with her sobs.

Finally, I feel her gently pushing back, and I realize how tightly I've been holding her. I let her look up at me, and I see her face swollen and red with sobbing. Her eyes are bloodshot, and she's looking at me as if she doesn't believe what she's seeing, like this is some kind of dream that she'll wake up from soon.

My face can't help but comfort her with a smile, and I brush some of her stray locks out of the way to see her better. When I broke out of prison a lifetime ago, I felt like the sight of her again was sweeter than anything I'd ever experience again.

The sight of her now proves me wrong.

"Luca," her thick voice manages. "You're...I...oh my god, you're alive!"

"Did you think a little thing like death could keep me from you?"

That earns me a smile from that gorgeous face of hers, ever so faint, still so tired, and she shakes her head, unable to hold back a laugh before she lets her forehead rest against my chest.

"Oh my god, Luca, this is...you're real, aren't you?"

"Real as you," I say, a few happy tears rolling down my face now as well. I let my arms go down to her arms, and I give her a gentle squeeze. "But it's sweeter than any dream I've ever had."

She sniffs and looks back up at me with shining eyes and a smile that's tired, so very tired, yet so happy. But then my smile drops and gives way to a look of concern. I take a step back, still holding her arms, and I look her up and down.

"Are you okay? Are you hurt? Did those *stronzi* lay a finger on you?" My blood is suddenly boiling all over again at the thought as my eyes rove over Serena for signs of wounds. The thought of any of those fucking monsters so much as looking at the love of my life, of them harming my child.

On instinct, my hand goes to her stomach to feel her, and I look up at Serena to meet her eyes as she lays one of her small, soft hands over my big one.

"I...I think I'm okay," she says with a soft nod. "We're okay, I mean," she adds, giving the hand over her belly a light squeeze to mean the baby.

"What happened at the shelter?" I ask, my tone soft yet serious. I need to know what the situation is with us right here, right now. I'm prepared to run immediately if we need to. Anything to keep Serena safe. "Were you followed?"

It takes her a moment to think about what I asked her, her eyes fluttering as she gives her head a little shake of confusion.

"We...we were attacked," she says, "I'm not sure what happened. The guy who was helping us out, he took me into some side room and told me to come here. I mean, I think it was here—it's dark, and I was scared and confused, and I-I-" she starts stammering, so I simply nod, running my hands through her hair with an understanding face.

"It's okay, you're safe now," I say as I hug her tight to me again. I can feel her fighting sobs as the recent memories come back to the surface.

"I don't think I was followed," she says into my shoulder, and I nod. "Oh my god, I the other women there, I..."

"They can handle things," I say. "This old ruin isn't the only contingency plan they have. That shelter has been here for a long time. Some punk-ass kids from the Bronx aren't going to shake them, but those punks couldn't be allowed to know exactly where you are or get a shot at harming you."

"So they *were* after me," she says, pulling back and looking up at my face. "This was all because of me?" She gives her head a little shake and asks, "For that matter, how on earth did *you* find me? How do you even know all this?"

"I have many skills," I say with a cocky smile, and her near-tears break down into a laugh as she slaps my chest.

"Jesus, it really is you," she says before sniffing. "But seriously."

God, it feels good to laugh with her again.

"A lot of people helped you get here," I say simply. "Many of them are my friends—and I might have been dead, but that didn't mean I couldn't keep an ear out when I needed to," I say with a wink. She doesn't look satisfied, but I give her a squeeze. "I'll explain more, but first, I think your nerves need a break. I can't imagine how much you've been through today." I glance around the room we're standing in. "How long have you been here?"

"I..." she starts, following my gaze. "Not long. I just staggered in here and kind of...collapsed," she says with a blushing face. I nod.

"That's fine, I wouldn't expect any more from anyone in your place." I give her a reassuring smile. "This place is a shit-hole, but there's a little more to it than meets the eye. Come on," I say, and before she can say anything, I stoop down and scoop her up off her feet, cradling her gently in my arms.

"Woah!" she says, surprised, but she laughs the next moment, putting her arms around my neck again. It's good to hold her again. "If you're sure," she says, swallowing. "What *is* this place, anyway?"

I start walking her toward a small set of stairs leading up. They've seen better days, and there's dust everywhere, but it'll do in a pinch.

"In New York, we have proper safehouses buried in the urban jungle," I explain. "This is Puglia—Apulia, as they call it in English—we don't have that kind of luxury. This is the next best thing to a safehouse."

"Hiding out in ruined villas in the countryside?"

"More or less. This part of the country has seen better days. There are ruins like this all over the place, and you have to be a local to know where most of them are—they don't show up on internet maps."

"So...we're really safe here?"

I frown. "Depends on whether the local mafia is working with the men hunting us. I don't plan on staying here long, but we can take a moment to breathe."

"Sounds about right," she says, and I smile at her.

"In any case, this place isn't exactly a vacation home, but it does have a few amenities you'll appreciate."

A few minutes later, we're standing in a roomy bathroom with black and white tiled floors. The tub looks antique, but it's in good enough shape to use.

"Don't worry, there *is* hot water," I say as I turn the shower on to start running water. Serena is standing behind me, and I can feel her gaze on me. I would bet I know what she's thinking, too.

So, as steam starts to rise from the water, I turn around and smile at her before lifting my tight shirt off my body. "I know you have questions. But we should get a little more comfortable while we talk about it, don't you think?"

Her eyes go up and down my hardened body, and I can almost see the tension melting from her as she looks at the familiar scars, the familiar contours of my form...everything she remembers. It's as if she weren't really sure it were me until she saw the roadmap of wounds left on me.

She smiles.

"I'd like that."

I step forward and take her hand gently, putting it to one of the scars on my side and letting her feel it. I want her to know that I'm here, for it to really sink in—and I know that isn't going to happen immediately.

"I...I'm sorry," she says, laughing at herself a little as she shakes her head. "I know it's silly, I just...I can't believe you're really here. I saw you get-"

I gently lift her chin up to look at my still face before I lean in and press my lips to hers. Instantly, my cock twitches and swells at the familiar warmth that I've craved so badly. It feels so *right*. Every second, every single moment the two of us are touching, it feels like we were made for each other. I can hear her breath get quick for a moment before she lets out a soft moan into the kiss.

When the kiss finally ends, I nod.

"I know. Let me help you with this," I say, putting my hands to her shirt. She moves her arms to let me lift it up and over her head. I toss it to the floor while my eyes fixate on her belly. She's showing, and she looks more beautiful than I could have dreamed of— and I did dream of her. Every single night, I dreamed of her.

My hand strokes her stomach, and a wide smile spreads across my face. "I can't believe it," I whisper.

"Me neither," she admits, looking down at the bump with me.

"I should have been with you," I say, an edge to my voice as I think about all the time I've spent away from my girl, away from my child. My hands reach around her back to undo her bra, and soon, it falls to the ground too. The sight of her whole bare torso, breasts and belly exposed, kindles something new in me.

There's a kind of beauty to my pregnant Serena that I can't explain. I feel the same desire for her, fanned stronger and hotter than ever, but there's a primal attraction to the sight of her that reaches some deep part of me I've never glimpsed before. It's intoxicating and fresh all at once.

"I've missed you so badly, Luca," she says as I unbutton her pants and let them slide down her legs, leaving her completely bare once she steps out of them. It doesn't take me long to get the rest of my clothes off, revealing the thick shaft between my legs, hanging half-swollen for her already.

I help her into the bathtub, and she sighs softly as the hot water runs down her body, washing away the whole painful day.

"We don't have any soap," I say, stepping close to her as she turns and looks up at me, "but water will do for now."

"I'm okay with that," she says softly as mist starts to hang in the room like a cloud. I smile, and my hands go to her shoulders, feeling the water pattering against our skin as I turn Serena around and run my hands down her sides.

My cock rests between her asscheeks as I explore her form, helping the water do its work as she leans back into me, resting her head against my chest.

"What happened back there, Luca?" she asks, and I know it's time to give her an explanation.

"I only remember patches of the night itself," I confess, my mind flashing back to it all. "I went to the car with one of the men. Fabio. He caught up with me and told me he's dinged my car a little when he was parking next to me—the poor man was a nervous wreck about telling me. But we'd both come in company cars, and he said he'd just had new speakers put into the one he drove, so he offered to swap cars so he could take mine to the shop to get touched up."

Serena puts her hands over mine, which have stopped at her hips. I stare at the wet tile walls as I remember that hellish night.

"Fabio was parked on the left of my car. We both went to our doors, and...it's patchy after that. Some car bombs go off when you open the door. That must have been what happened, because the next thing I remember, I was on the ground, my ears were ringing, and everything stung bitterly. I had glass and metal in me. The pain was so intense I felt myself slipping in and out from the very start. The bullets flying overhead sounded dull, I was so deaf-ened. Our cars are reinforced to resist bullets—if there hadn't been that armored car between us..."

I pause for a moment. I had remembered enough to look over to where Fabio had been standing. He had just...ceased to exist.

"How did you get out of there?" she asks.

"The Cleaners weren't expecting resistance," I say. "My men were on me in a few seconds. I remember seeing a friendly face. It might have been Nico, but I can't remember. The last thing I said was to get you out of there, far, far away. Whoever I said that to knew what I meant."

"You had me sent here," she says. I give her a light squeeze and kiss her neck softly.

"America wasn't safe for you, Serena," I say. "This is the only place I know far enough away that it would at least buy me time."

"I thought you were dead... all these months," she says with a pain straining her throat.

"If I'd had a say in it, I would have been with you the whole time," I say, and it's the truth. I bring her hand to my scars again...the new ones as well as the old. "I woke up with one of the family's surgeons. He had me medicated while he treated me for...I don't know how long. Too long. I must have had more shrapnel in me than I realized. Broken ribs. All I could do was dream of you."

"Luca..."

"The first time I was fully conscious, I woke up to more stitches in me than I'd ever had before. But the Cleaners must have caught up to my trail by then, because that same day, one of their men showed up. Killed the doctor before I could get the IVs out of me and tear him apart." I look to some of the fresher wounds on my upper arm. "I knew it was going to be a rough recovery, but I couldn't stay there any longer. I got in touch with Raf and headed off to catch up with you. I still know the layout out here, and the contingency plans like this villa. I had to be careful to look for you quietly, but I couldn't leave you alone."

Serena turns around and looks up at me with big eyes. The water starts dousing her hair, getting it soaking wet and letting it hang on her shoulders like vines. I put my hands around her face, running my thumb over her lower lip as water patters off her and onto my face.

"The whole time I thought you were gone, I didn't know how I was going to keep going," she says, but her hand goes to her stomach as she looks down briefly. "Having some of you with me helped." She smiles as she looks down at what's going to be our child, looking absolutely radiant. "The baby is going to be as strong as you, Luca. I know it."

I put my forehead to hers, my heart swelling with pride.

"*Si, passerotta mia,* but it will get its strength from you."

She looks up at me and locks her lips with mine, and I feel myself swell so stiff that my cock touches her, pressing in, desperate to feel her warmth again. She draws in a sharp breath at the mere feeling of it, and I can tell that her body craves me every bit as much.

"I have a lot of time to make up for," I say as my hands go to her breasts, thumbs stroking over her hardening nipples. Water runs between us softly, warming us to each other even more.

"Yes you do," she practically purrs, pressing herself up against me. "Fuck, I've wanted you so badly, Luca."

"You've been through a lot," my voice rumbles, but even as I say so, we walk backward until she's pressed against the cool tile. "I can hardly keep my hands off you, but if you need to rest-"

I feel Serena's hand grip my cock firmly, and the mere feeling of her hand running up its length to the crown and lingering on my tip makes it rock-hard, desperate for her, the pressure in my groin so full and ready for her that it's almost painful.

Those playful eyes of hers are alive again with the very red-hot energy I fell in love with so long ago, lidded by long lashes.

"The only thing I need right now, Luca," she whispers, putting a hand on my chest and running her fingernails down it, "is you. Inside me. Now."

Feeling him grip me is like being in a giant's arms, and the easy strength he uses to pull me in and bring his lips to mine makes me feel safe for the first time in what feels like a lifetime.

It's strange, a grip like that, firm and powerful, should make me feel like he's taking control of me, taking everything into his hands. But I've spent so long on the run in other people's hands, hiding from place to place. I don't want that feeling anymore. And with Luca, somehow, being in his embrace helps me feel like I'm standing on my own two feet for the first time.

He's not another set of arms to hold me. He's my shelter in this storm.

I sigh into his kiss as the hot water rolls over my shoulder. It's so hot it almost scalds me, but his hands still feel warmer. And I'm feeling even warmer between my legs. That groan that rumbles in his chest, full of desire and strength...it's everything I've dreamed of. It's that sound, that feeling that's stayed alive in the back of my mind.

I still can't believe it's him. Seeing him at all after what happens defies all odds, all my expectations.

But really, that's what our whole relationship has been: against all odds.

I let Luca walk me backward in the shower, gently, until I'm pressed up against the cool tile wall. The room is so steamy that it's not icy, but it sends a thrilling shiver down my back. My heart is pounding, and I feel excitement welling up in me so hard that I'd be shaking if it weren't like a sauna in here.

My eyes slowly shut as I feel Luca start to explore my body. It feels like he's discovering everything all over again. His hands slide around my hips to my ass first, squeezing it gently at first. I give him a little thrust of my hips to ask for more, and wordlessly, he understands. The next moment, he pushes back into me and pinches me on my ass enough that I gasp into his kiss.

He silences me with his tongue. I feel it delve into my mouth, his rough stubble brushing against my face slightly. Fuck, I already feel so tense inside, ready to explode at a moment's notice. I can't hold myself back any longer.

My hands go up to his chest, and my nails dig

into his flesh, running down those rippling, tight pectoral muscles, down to his abs. I'd count them if my head weren't so dizzy with need. Another shiver runs up my body, but not from the cold—this time, it's like old sensations I thought dead forever coming back to life. My body remembers everything about him, everything about the passionate seconds we passed together.

And it's desperate for more.

I crave him, every inch of him. My fingers run down his dark skin until they reach the V leading to his groin, and soon, my hands have found that thick, wet shaft that's as hot and ready as I am. It's pointed up toward me, resting against me, grinding against me every time one of us moves. I feel it harden and pulse at the same time that I feel my pussy wetten and warm in anticipation.

"I've missed you so fucking much," I gasp when our kiss breaks, and I tilt my head back to rest against the tile as his mouth goes to my exposed neck. We started gentle, but we're realizing that after so long apart...neither of us knows how long we can hold ourselves back before this turns into something more savage.

And that's something I think we're both eager for.

His teeth graze my neck at first, brushing against it with the stubble of his cheeks. Then I feel a nip, and I gasp. He presses himself in closer, and his hands grip my hips tighter as he starts to rub himself against me. The feeling of his teeth gently on my neck gets more aggressive, and I can feel that huge, strong heart of his thumping in his chest as he hugs me against his pecs.

He grips me possessively because he knows I'm his, even though we've been apart so long. My breathing is hot and fast as my lips hang open, water running in little streams down my face as I feel my whole body twitch with need for him.

He moves his hands to my back and claws me, running those rough carpenter's hands down my spine, feeling every inch of my smooth skin. His hands run down to my ass, where he rubs his palms into my cheeks, massaging me and groping me. His cock pulses with every new part of me he touches.

His body is powerful and built better than anyone I've met in my life. It's incredible to know that all that strength can get excited just by the touch of me—just by the *thought* of me.

"Serena," he groans in a husky voice, lips by my ear as he leaves my poor neck alone at last. "I told you I'd never leave you. Did you think I'd make a liar of myself?"

I'm too breathy to respond, and he nips my ear, making me whimper and squirm in his grip.

I can't take it any longer.

My hands go to his cock again and start running up and down its length. My eyes flutter open to meet his. The sight of his face there—steam all around us, his dark eyes piercing into my soul, water running down his short hair and those features that look like they were cut from the finest marble—makes my heart flutter. He could hold me paralyzed with that look.

His face cracks that boyish smile. My Luca. My own Luca.

He clenches his teeth a moment as my fingers run up his cock and my thumb brushes the tip. I can electrify him with just a touch of my hand, and that knowledge makes my heart soar.

"You're always playing with fire, *passerotta mia*," he whispers as his hand runs from my hip to my thigh, still strong and firm as ever, and I have barely enough time to brace myself before he hoists me up just enough to impale me on his cock.

I let out a scream that he silences with a kiss. Neither of us want to be slow anymore. We can't take it, and the steam between us is only making us more and more worked up. We finally have all the time in the world, and damn it, I'm going to take advantage of that.

The feeling of that huge, familiar shaft entering me is unbelievable. It's as if my whole body were stretching out and feeling a swirl of relief all concentrated between my legs. It's hot and intense, stretching me taut and wringing me out all in the same feeling.

The water is hot, but I feel hot tears running from my face too. It's not pain—my pussy is so needy and so ready for him that he feels nothing but incredible in me—it's the overwhelming feeling of knowing that we're together again.

My inner depths pulse with ecstasy as his cock gets flooded with my honey. His tongue plunges into my mouth, and while one hand helps hold me up, his free hand goes to my left breast, groping me and rolling his thumb over the hard, stiff nub. I'm aching for him, and he holds nothing back.

Immediately, he starts thrusting up into me. We're in sync as if we'd never spent a single night apart. His hips move back and forth as I let my head roll back, his mouth going to my neck and ravishing the exposed flesh, then moving down to the nape.

I'm like a doll in his hands. My hair is soaking wet, and after he's had his fun toying with my nipple and getting it stiffer than ever, his hand goes to my back and takes a handful of it. The grip he has on me just makes me feel all the tighter, blissfully strung out in Luca's hands.

Each time he thrusts, his cock solid as a rock and pulsing with desire, I feel electricity run from the walls of my pussy up into the rest of my groin, then further up to tighten in my lower abdomen. From there, I feel every nerve in my body begging me not to let this stop.

I rock my hips in time with him, but even if I

wanted to just lay back and enjoy it, Luca could have handled it. He bucks back and forth at a steady rhythm, not going too deep to hurt me but filling up every inch of what he explores of me.

"Serena," he breathes into my ears. He's practically panting, growling my name. "Serena, fuck, I want to feel you come on my cock. I want you to do that for me, baby."

"Oh god," I gasp, needing no encouragement. "Luca, I...I'm so close, please don't stop!"

He's a machine. I don't know how he's holding me up this way or how he can keep himself moving like this after whatever he must have gone through to find me all the way out here, but I would rather die than let it stop now.

Something wells up inside me, and I scramble to get my hands on his biceps to hold myself up. I feel so tight inside that I'm afraid I might lose control of myself and start convulsing, so I need something, anything to hold onto. I feel his biceps, but they're too thick and hard to get a good grip on. I whimper in desperation as I feel Luca hurdling me toward the point of no return, and just when I think I'm about to lose myself, Luca pushes me back and up against the wall just as I can't contain myself anymore.

He thrusts up deeper than ever as I come, and I let out a sharp, short squeak that melts into a long, ragged sigh while my body is pinned between the tile and Luca's hot body. After my limbs twitch and I feel my honey warming his cock and mixing with his precome, his cock pulsing inside me, I realize he's holding me up entirely. I've lost control of my body, and Luca is holding my limp form up with his strong arms and that solid dick that's just as desperate for release.

"I want you to come in me, Luca," I manage, afterglow radiating around me like a halo. "Please, I want to feel you fill me up, it's been so long!"

"Soon, *carissima*," he teases me, putting a finger to my chin and lifting my face up for him to kiss. It's sweet and short, and right now, it's the sweetest thing I could possibly taste. His tone turns dark when he leans in to whisper into my ear, "I'm not done making up for lost time yet."

Slowly, he draws his cock out of me, and I immediately try to push my hips back into it. I feel like I'm missing something without it in me, and I whimper in protest, gripping his biceps pleadingly. Luca must have noticed, because he chuckles, brushing a little strand of wet hair out of my eyes and kissing me again to pacify me while he slides out. "Patience," he urges me through that wicked grin of his.

"I need you in me," I say, feeling relaxation from head to toe already, a relaxation that's almost *heavy* on me like an aura. I sound stupid, but god, it's the truest thing I can say right now.

"I can't deny you anything, you know that," he growls just before he turns me around. I catch myself with my hands against the tile. He takes hold of my hips, perching his cock on the surface of my pussy as he takes his time groping my ass, his chest giving a low rumble as he savors the feeling of it.

"This, Serena," he says with a quick, wet slap of my ass that makes me whimper and wiggle my hips, begging him to spear me. "This could bring me back from the dead."

I don't have time to answer before he thrusts up into me. My fingers try to clench, but the tile keeps me pinned against the wall, my mouth hanging open as I feel warmth roil through my body in an entirely new way. His cock his long and thick, but just changing positions electrifies new parts of my body, reminds me of so much of what I've been missing.

Both of his massive hands reach around to grope my front, first cupping my breasts and squeezing, toying with them, flicking the hardening nipples with his thumbs and running his fingers teasingly over my areolas. I can feel every ridge of his cock inside me, ribbed with veins, pulsing with every motion.

He starts rocking steadily again, letting me take a breath so as not to overwhelm me with the sensation. But I can tell he isn't going to go easy on me—not by a long shot.

Even when I think back to all the passionate nights we've spent together, I don't know if I've ever felt him this taut and ready, so swollen, so...*huge*. His balls don't hit me in this position, but I can still feel their weight as they swing under us in the shower. He's swollen with need for me, and the thought of him unleashing himself inside of me is enough to warm me up inside all over again.

The way the past few weeks have been going, sex has been the last thing on my mind. So this overwhelming presence of Luca all around me, inside me, filling me up, it all hits me like a truck out of nowhere. It's thrilling and relaxing all at once, like a medicine I didn't even realize I needed.

I feel the bulging crown of his cock inside of me grinding against me as he moves in and out, and soon, I feel my body electrifying as he reaches my g-spot. My whole body starts to tense, and I know he can feel it—I clench around him to make sure he feels, because I want Luca to share every second of this ecstasy I'm feeling.

His cock feels like it's white-hot against my insides, and I put my forehead against the wet tile wall so it doesn't fall over. I feel like jelly in his hands. Just as I'm starting to lose myself entirely in his steady, rhythmic pace that's picking right up to what it was a few moments ago, I feel one of his hands start to wander further down, away from my breast.

My pussy tightens in anticipation as Luca's strong, gentle fingers make their way to my clit. As soon as I feel his rough fingertip on my sensitive, swollen nub, he has to hold me up again as my legs shake, another orgasm crashing through me.

My body has been totally awakened to him, and the orgasms come more freely now. My panting breaths go in time with his thrusts. His tip strikes my g-spot while his fingers swirl around my clit, and I lose track of time in the rush of it all. I'm hardly aware that there's even water falling on us anymore. All I can feel is the swelling rhythm of my orgasms as his steady, pounding rhythm drives me home over and over again.

My body tensing up gradually and then relaxing with a beautiful, wonderful shudder is the only thing I use to measure time anymore. Just the feeling of Luca's hands around me again is almost as wonderful as the overwhelming feeling I have in every inch of my body.

I start to get a better footing in the tub, and Luca starts rubbing his hands up and down my body, really exploring me as if it's for the first time again. It hits me why I feel so unbelievably safe with Luca, despite all the danger that seems to follow us around. He loves me in a way that makes every second touching me worthwhile. I can feel it in his hands on my hips, on my stomach, on my breasts. He loves me, body and soul, the same way I love him.

Tears are running down my face again, and my eyes pop open when he slides out of me suddenly. I turn my head to look at him, but he's already grabbing my face and bringing me into a deep, hungry kiss at the same time he drives his cock into me.

We're locked in a long, deep kiss as he starts thrusting faster, and this time, I recognize the way he's losing his rhythm, the way he's starting to grab me like he's holding me to him. There's something brutal and animalistic to it, every bit as fierce as he is sweet, all in the same storm of feelings that he fans up in me.

I'm hopelessly, deeply in love with him, and my whole body roars up as one to join him when I feel his cock starting to tense up harder, balls tightening, bucking getting wild—never careless, but wild.

He spreads my arms out outstretched on the tile and holds me by the wrists as he pounds. He's leaving me totally exposed to him, unable to stop him as he tilts his head back and lets out a deep, ragged groan...

The feeling of his seed bursting into me is the most exciting and comforting feeling I've felt since...since...I can't even remember. It's all just a golden, dizzy blur as shot after shot of hot come washes my insides with Luca. He pours himself out into me entirely, and I feel filled with life all over again. I realize I'm smiling in the shower, hot water getting in my mouth as I almost want to laugh. My head is getting giddy, sensations so jumbled up and wonderful as we come together that I feel out of control of myself.

All I know is that I'm happy. Luca has me, he's coming in me, and we belong to each other. In my wildest dreams, I never could have thought that would be how tonight would end up. When I open my eyes once we've stopped moving, I'm half-expecting him to not be there. That this was all just a dream, or even the afterlife.

But Luca's still there, glowing as much as I am with that damned cocky smile on his face.

"Is this for real?" I let spill from my mouth. "I mean, are you a dream or something?"

"*Dolcezza*," he says, putting a hand to my cheek, "I've been asking myself that this whole time."

A few minutes later, Luca has dried me off with a towel that's a little too stiff for my liking, but beggars can't be choosers. We start to walk out of the bathroom, but I realize my legs are shaking too much from the...well, the everything.

Giggling, I'm swept off my feet by Luca before he carries me out the door and up to a modest little bedroom on the same floor.

"This place must have been nice when it was still lived in," I say as he sets me down beside a bed that isn't too gnarly, but it's seen better days, and the sheets smell a little like dust.

"Some of them are still in use," he says as he fluffs the pillows a little. "I'll have to show you one some-day. For now, though, you'll have to take my word for it," he adds with a wink. "I've got some supplies I brought with me—I have a vehicle. We can eat light in the morning and get a move on. For now, though," he says, walking over to me and helping me get into the sheets. My eyelids got heavy all of the sudden.

Not that I should be surprised. All that adrenaline was bound to crash sometime soon.

"You need some rest," Luca says, sitting on the bed next to me with a warm smile as I beam up at him, bundling sheets around myself. I don't even care that the bed is stiff—I would sleep on a pile of hay at this point.

"That sounds…" I try to say before I yawn, and I feel sleep overtaking me like a warm bath.

Luca's smile splits into a grin, and he says something that makes my heart flutter, but I'm already falling deep into sleep.

…And the next thing I'm aware of, god knows how many hours later, is his hand on my shoulder and his deep voice in my ear. But it's not the warm and comforting sound I was expecting—it sounds urgent. I fight off the sleep all around me and look at his blurry face and his moving mouth. The look in his eyes tells me everything I need to know.

"We have to go. Now."

I heard them coming from a long way away. Sound travels farther in this landscape than many foreigners realize. And I heard cars. Several of them.

When Serena dozed off to sleep, I had been keeping watch. It was hard to tear my eyes away from that peaceful form, watching her chest rise and fall as her small hand rests on the tiny bump of her belly. Even in the midst of a storm, she's as peaceful as can be.

Exhaustion will do that.

I only had two guns on me when I came into the villa to meet her in case she'd been followed or worse, so as soon as she'd dozed off, I went back to my vehicle to get a little more gear: spare guns and a knife, as well as a set of clothes in case we made it to the morning undisturbed. I have a set of binoculars, but out here in the near pitch-black of the Apulian night, you can see a set of headlights from a long, long way away, and nobody would dare try to handle these roads with the lights out.

And when I spotted the headlights, it was about half an hour before sunrise. I wasted no time.

Serena gets out of bed quickly, snapping awake almost instantly despite how deeply she'd been down. Within less than a minute, she's gotten up and pulled enough clothes on to move while I watch the window.

"How close are they?" she asks, concern in her voice. It makes my heart sink to know she's had to harden herself this much. No woman like her deserves to have to get used to such violence.

"There's nobody else on the roads this early," I say. "They're closer than I'd like, let's leave it at that."

"Right."

We rush down the stairs, and I already have one gun out while my other hand holds Serena's. I'm not going to let anything separate us while we're getting out of here. Not when we've just been brought back together.

By the time I throw the door open, I can already see headlights on the road as the vehicles hurdle closer toward us. I feel Serena's hand clench mine, and on instinct, I draw her under my arm as I help her run with me.

"Keep your head low," I command, and I ready my pistol as we rush toward my own vehicle.

It's a rough-and-tumble SUV that looks like it could withstand its fair share of action, because I came here planning for that. It's big and it's tough: two things that can be rare and valuable in a car for Southern Italian driving.

It's also a rental. Despite the insurance, I don't have much hope I'll be able to return it.

But even as we dart to the SUV, several sedans roar into view, all black, all tinted windows, and some of those windows rolling down.

We have a matter of seconds before hell breaks loose.

I turn so that Serena is hidden by my bulk, and I raise my weapon. My only armor consists of a tight white t-shirt and black jeans, meaning we need to get to the car *now*. I fire a few rounds that spark off the cars, and they start veering off to the side, both to get out of the line of fire and to get better shots at me. Serena doesn't scream, she just tries to make herself small as we race to the car. She's been through enough by now that she's started to harden herself against fear.

Gunshots start ringing out into the humid night air. I *feel* them whizzing too close to us for comfort. I duck down with Serena as we cross the rocky way to the door as I hear the shots ricocheting off the villa behind us, bits of decades-old stone chipping away.

I return fire, and my aim is deadly. I'm not interested in just causing a distraction. These men dare try to harm my Serena and my child, so I shoot to kill.

Glass from the tinted windows shatters as I fire at them with one hand while using the other to move Serena behind me once we reach the car. With me covering her, she opens the car and crawls into the passenger's seat. Once she's in and crouched down, I duck under the front of the car and hurry to the other side, blind-firing a couple of rounds from the corner before popping out and getting into the driver's seat.

We hear bullets ping off the edge of the car as I turn the engine on, throw the SUV into gear, and peel around harder than I've ever taken this thing. Dirt gets kicked up as I do a half-circle around the unpaved space that passes for a driveway in front of the villa before I roar toward the exit.

Two of the sedans had parked in front of the entryway to keep me from doing just that, but I head for the outer edge of the left one and throw my brights on to let him know he has about five seconds to decide to move.

I can see a pair of widening white eyes in the driver's seat as the man drops his gun and makes the wise choice to throw his car into reverse. I still scrape the front of his car as I tear out of there and onto the road, and I can already hear the engines roaring after us.

And I keep going past it, right off the road on the other side, into the brush.

"Oh my god what are you doing!" Serena gasps all in one breath, bracing herself with all four limbs in the passenger's seat with equally wide eyes.

"Hang tight," I say, checking the rear-view mirror as I change gears to get my vehicle *really* moving. "If these boys want us so badly, they can try to come after us."

"It's all rocks and trees out there though!"

"Exactly."

I don't have to look over to know Serena's looking at me like I'm crazy. I just cock an eyebrow and dart my eyes in her direction for a half-second to add, "Buckle up."

Serena scrambles to get the strap over her chest as I weave through a small grove of olive trees that have long since been abandoned and started to grow wild. Behind me, I see lights starting to come back into view.

I crack a smile. So they really do have a backbone.

"Why not just take the road?!" Serena asks as she steals a glance behind us. But the next moment, we can both hear the gunshots, so she ducks back down to where she was a moment ago.

"I counted five cars back there," I say, taking a sharp turn around a large boulder jutting out of the ground, dust flying up behind us. The ground is getting drier as we get further out. This part of Italy isn't that different from the landscape of the American West. "If we were on the open road with this monster of an SUV, it would be the easiest thing in the world for them to get us boxed in and pepper us with bullets."

Serena winces as we hear another bullet hit the back of the car, so I start veering right through some rocky terrain that would be hell on the tires of any other car.

"I know this landscape," I explain. "These boys that are after us? My bet is they're kids from the Bronx. Hardened killers, maybe, but not even the best of the best from New York know how to handle off-road driving like this."

Serena opens her mouth to speak again, but the loud sound of a car crashing against one of the trees behind us distracts her. I reach over and put my hand on her knee, giving it a gentle squeeze.

"Don't you worry—I haven't let myself forget the terrain out here."

Serena gives me a nervous smile, and that's enough for me.

I veer into some hills, and a quick glance behind me tells me there are still three of them. I heard one crash, and the other must have chickened out or lost a tire trying to come after us.

Barreling through the darkness, I wind through dried-out shrubs, twisted and dead trees, piles of rocks, and craggy, low cliffs. Turning around the corner of another ruined villa that's in worse shape than the safehouse, another one of the sedans chasing us doesn't clear the turn and tumbles over in a storm of dust.

That doesn't give us a moment to rest, though.

"Shit," I grunt as I look ahead of us. We're headed for a wide-open field. Judging from the rows of dirt and overgrown weeds, this used to be someone's homestead farm, long ago. And there's no cover anywhere to be seen.

"There's two more of them," Serena says, an anxious edge in her voice.

"Don't worry," I assure her. "But do hang on. I mean it this time," I add as I roll the window down.

"What?"

The next moment, I slam the brakes and turn the car sharply to face the oncoming cars, which veer to each side to try to avoid me. But my gun is already out, and I fire at the one on my left four times, right at the driver's side.

Its car horn starts blaring as the driver's body slumps forward and the car keeps spinning in a circle in the field.

I take advantage of the confusion—the other car tries to spin back around, but the car I shot at blocks its way while the passengers try to get the dead driver off the gas. It gives me all the time I need to rocket into the opposite direction, clearing the field.

"*Holy shit, Luca!*" Serena breathes.

"Are you okay?" I ask, looking at her seriously for a moment. She gives me an incredulous look, and it takes her a moment to just nod. "Y-yeah, fine. Where did you learn how to drive like this?"

"Look, there's not a lot to do out here," I say with a smug grin on my face as I glance into the rear-view mirror and see the other cars just now managing to get back on my tail. "When you're a boy with a bunch of friends and one of them has a beat-up car and some time to kill, well...it's a better way to pass the time than bare-knuckle boxing, right?"

"I mean…"

"We did that too, though," I admit before I veer off toward some dunes, and Serena yelps as the car takes a sudden dip.

Behind us, I can see the sun peaking up over the horizon, just starting to cast light over the landscape. We must have been driving out here for nearly an hour already.

My car can handle the small ditches and dunes the rough landscape has with ease that the shiny sedans behind us couldn't hope to match. For once, having the sleekest and fastest cars isn't an advantage. Still, I know it's only a matter of time before they decide to try something else, so I need to get creative.

I drive us past the dunes toward what looks like a ruinous pile of rocks to the west of us.

"What *is* all that?" Serena asks, leaning forward and squinting.

"Many, many years ago, it was a village," I say as we get closer. There are strange, round buildings with roofs that look like pointy pyramid cones and piles of stones all around them, along with scrap metal, broken-down cars, and even the odd rusty washing machine here and there. "Now, it's a scrap yard for some other village nearby. Those buildings are called *trulli*."

"Why are we driving toward them?"

"They're sturdier than they look," I say with a smile. Serena knows what that means by now, so she braces herself as I whip the car into the run-down ghost town and use the hand brake to help me around one of the little round buildings.

Before they even enter the village proper, the car whose driver I shot hits a ditch on the way in and gets stuck, pinned between a mound of dirt and someone's broken washing machine, spinning wheels sending a cloud of dirt flying up around it.

The final car makes it a little further, barreling after us as someone leans out the passenger window with a gun in hand to try to take aim at us.

But *trulli* are a little unusual in their layout, and it takes them by surprise to try to drive around a clump of them, only to find the row of houses extending farther than one would expect. The car slams on the brakes, but it careens into the stone buildings, endless stones from the roof collapsing over the car while the vehicle crumples against the stone wall.

We drive off, zipping through an old hazelnut grove to the blissful sound of nobody roaring after us. All I can hear besides the hum of the engine is Serena breathing for a few minutes, looking into the rear-view mirrors every few seconds to make sure there aren't any of them left.

When it's safe enough not to tempt fate anymore, she says, "Are...are they gone?"

"If any of them can catch up to us after the ride I took them on," I say, taking a deep breath and leaning back in my seat, "then they've earned a proper fight."

Serena looks like she's tense at that, and I chuckle, taking out my aviator sunglasses from the glove box and popping them on. "I'm kidding, *dolcezza*."

"Fuck you," she laughs, a nervous yet relieved laugh that lets her lean back in her seat too as we ride into the sunrise.

After a little ways further on the rocky off-road terrain, I bring us back onto the road. The highways out here are dirty and half-falling apart, but after the ride we've been on, even a rough road is a welcome feeling.

Ten minutes later, we're heading southward on the road, and it's taken us up onto a high hill that gives us a far and wide view of the area. With the sunrise peaking over the horizon, it's a gorgeous view, and my heart swells with pride to see Serena looking out the window.

Golden rays of sunlight touch groves and farmland for miles, cypress trees swaying in the distance as a gentle breeze blesses the landscape. The smell of early springtime flowers is in the air that whips around us.

"It might not be upstate New York," I say with a little fake humility, "but it's something, isn't it?"

"Yeah…" she says wistfully, a smile on her face. "I never knew all this was out here. It makes me…" She pauses, and her smile fades. "Nauseous."

I blink. "What?"

"No, I mean I need to throw up. Can you pull over?" She puts a hand to her chest and bites her lip, and immediately, I bring us to the side of the road and stop the car so Serena can hurry out and retch. I get out of my side immediately, my heart pounding —had she been hit? Was the strain too much? Is it just motion sickness?

Oh, wait, shit—morning sickness.

I come around the side of the car to Serena and put my hand on her back. "Take your time," I say, not sure how to comfort her but doing my best. "Nobody's out here this early."

"Oh god, don't look at me like this!" she half-laughs before being sick again.

"You've seen me in worse ways," I say with a grin, and when she finishes and turns to give me a weak smile, she sees me holding a towel, a bottle of water, and a little mouthwash for her.

"Wow, you came prepared, huh?"

"Traveling light doesn't mean forgetting the essentials," I say with a wink.

Serena cleans herself up while I help her, and after she spits the mouthwash out onto the ground, she takes a breath and gets back into the car.

As we pull off again, I'm quiet for a moment before I speak.

"I wish I could have been with you for more of this," I say, nodding to her. "The sickness, I mean. It's not easy to go through alone, let alone on the run like this."

"Me too," she says softly.

"How much longer do you have with that? Does it last the whole pregnancy?"

"I'm not sure—but no, they say it ends after about two and a half months," she says, furrowing her eyebrows. "But if I'm doing math in my head right, it shouldn't be too much longer? I'm not sure."

"Well, let's not worry about it right this second," I say, taking a turn onto a long road into a residential area. "We'll have time for that later."

We drive past a few modest houses and back

onto a strip of mostly uninhabited road that takes us past some wild trees and rocks before a short bend. Past that, up on a small hill that looks so much smaller now than when I first left it, I see the sight that I've been waiting years to lay eyes on again.

Serena leans forward in her seat to look at it as I pull the SUV to a stop. It's a modest villa, large enough for a single family, mostly made of white stone with a little terraced garden out the side by a porch with laundry strung up to dry. There are a few palm trees swaying in the breeze outside it, and there's a single car out front.

"Um…" Serena says as I turn the engine off and step out of the car, gesturing for her to follow with a smile. She does, but she looks up at the villa with confusion on her face before I come to slip my arm around her and hug her to my side.

"Why are we stopping here? What is this place, Luca?" she asks, smiling as I give her a gentle squeeze. When I reply, I can feel a lump in my throat.

"Home."

As we walk up the steps to the clean white villa, my stomach turns again and again. I will my body to chill the hell out, let me have a calm moment for once. But between the pregnancy hormones, the car chase, and of course the rush of being reunited with Luca, I'm not feeling very well at all. Luca takes my hand, giving me a look of reassurance before knocking on the door. The porch lamp flickers on above our heads, washing us in pale golden light. I look sideways at Luca, still in shock that he's alive. I can't believe it. He's really here. With me.

I still keep expecting to wake up and realize with a pit in my stomach that it was all just a happy dream, another fantasy to confuse my brain and make me wish for things that aren't true. But he squeezes my hand and smiles and I tell myself that this *is* real. This is really happening.

Luca said this place was home, but I'm not entirely sure what he means by that.

Until the door opens to reveal a teenage girl, probably about seventeen, sitting in a wheelchair looking very sleepy. It *is* early in the morning, after all. Then her big green eyes light up and a look of revelation appears on her face. The color drains from her cheeks and her mouth falls open, gaping at us—but more specifically, at Luca. She mutters something to herself, shaking her head slowly as she stares at him. Luca, meanwhile, is beaming brilliantly. There might even be just the slightest sheen of tears in his eyes.

The teenage girl murmurs, "B-Luca? *Sei tu?*"

He nods. "*Si. Ciao*, Domenica."

She shouts over her shoulder, down the hallway behind her, "Papa! Mama! *Vieni!*"

She quickly waves for us to come in, rolling her wheelchair back out of the way so we can close the door behind us. The girl reaches up to take Luca's hand, tugging him down to give him a tight hug. There's a big grin on her pretty face, and it looks very much like Luca's smile.

He kisses her on the forehead and mutters, "*La mia bella sorella.*"

Just then, a middle-aged couple comes trudging down the hallway. There's a tall, broad-shouldered man with a proud, handsome face and thick salt-and-pepper hair, and at his side is a much shorter woman with chin-length, smooth black hair, luminous green eyes, and frown lines etched into her face. But at the sight of Luca, both of them stop in place. They stare at him with the same wide-eyed, slack-jawed surprise the teenage girl did.

"*Luca, è possibile?*" asks the woman, raising a hand to her cheek in awe.

Beside me, Luca nods. The older man steps forward, shaking his head. He reaches out to touch Luca's chin, then his jaw and cheek, almost like he can't believe his own eyes. Like Luca might just disappear into thin air at any moment. I know the feeling. It's the same way I feel when I look at him, touch him. That's just the effect he has on people. Once you meet him and really get to know him, you're constantly worried that you might lose him.

"*Papa, sono io,*" he says, nodding. "*Veramente.*"

"*Mio figlio!*" the older man exclaims, throwing his arms around Luca in a hug. The woman comes shuffling over to hug them both, her beautiful face crumpling into happy tears.

So this is Luca's family, the ones I've heard bits and pieces about, the ones who sent him away to America in hopes of giving him a better life, a chance at escaping the temptation of joining a criminal gang here in Apulia.

I stand aside, overwhelmed but content to watch

the heartwarming scene unfold. The time will come to introduce me, but I'm not about to intrude on this golden moment.

The teenage girl looks at me suddenly, an expression of surprise on her face, like she's just noticing me for the very first time. She cocks her head to one side and says, *"Chi sei?"*

I answer her in Italian, hoping I can keep up with these fluent native speakers. "My name is Serena. I'm Luca's… um…"

"My fiancée," Luca intercepts in Italian. "Mama, Papa, Domenica—this is Serena De Laurentis. We met in New York when we were teenagers. I have loved her since the first day I saw her. She's come a long, long way to be here with me. With you."

I give them all a sheepish smile. It's been a long time since I've been introduced to someone's family, and never in a foreign language I can only speak with some small degree of fluency. I can get by, but I have a feeling I might fall behind if they start talking rapidly.

And of course, as soon as that thought crosses my mind, they all launch into one big hailstorm of rapid-fire questions and comments. They ask about how we met, how long I've been in Italy, who my parents are, where I come from. Am I hungry? Thirsty? Tired?

Once they take notice of my hand resting on my

stomach, the topic switches gear and gains even more intensity. Am I pregnant? Are they going to have a grandchild? How far along am I? How do I feel? Have I been drinking enough milk? Is it a boy or a girl?

"Slow down," Luca interrupts, laughing. "There will be plenty of time to ask all the questions you want, but for now I think Serena might like to sit down and get comfortable. We have had a rough time getting here. Lots of travel."

Luca's mother rushes over to take my arm. I'm not an incredibly tall person, but next to her I feel like a giant. She's barely over five feet tall, and I find myself wondering how funny it would be if Luca had inherited his mother's height rather than his father's. Mrs. Lomaglio leads me into a little sitting room down the hallway, plopping me down on a cushy red couch before hurrying off to the kitchen. Luca, Domenica, and Mr. Lomaglio come in after us.

Mrs. Lomaglio comes back quickly with a cup of something warm and vaguely sweet. Maybe some kind of tea. I've never been much of a tea-drinker, but I'm not about to refuse anything this sweet woman offers me, so I gladly take a sip. She smiles broadly, pleased.

"Is there anything else you'd like? Fruit? Cheese?" she asks.

"Hard cheeses only, Mama!" Domenica interjects

meaningfully. She looks back at me, blushing. "I'm studying to be a doctor. I take online classes."

"Oh, that's wonderful," I tell her. She looks positively joyful.

"Domenica has always been the smart one, even when she was little," Luca says.

"Both my children are brilliant," boasts Mrs. Lomaglio, getting up to get me some hard cheese and fruit from the kitchen. "Coffee, Luca?" she adds.

"*Si*, Mama. *Grazie*."

"I cannot believe it," says Mr. Lomaglio in his gruff, deep voice. I can tell he's a man of few words, keeping his thoughts to himself while his wife and daughter chatter away. "My son, come back to me after all this time."

"Of course, Papa. I couldn't stay away forever," Luca answers gently. "I would have come back sooner if I could. You know that."

His father nods very slowly, his jaw tightening as though he's trying desperately to keep from showing too much emotion. "What a fantastic surprise to see you again."

Mrs. Lomaglio comes back with a little silver tray of olives, grapes, diced pears, and what looks like long, triangular slices of either parmigiano or asiago. She sets the tray down on the little coffee table in front of Luca and me, and as much as I want to be a courteous, dainty houseguest, my pregnant stomach growls impatiently. I quickly start eating, munching happily while Luca catches up with his family. All the while, Mrs. Lomaglio glances at me with approval, like it gives her immense joy to watch me stuff my face.

"I'm surprised you remembered me so quickly," Luca says to his little sister, who is sitting with her hands folded in her lap. She shrugs and smiles.

"I may have been a little girl when you left, but I could never forget my big brother," she says warmly. "I cried so much when you went away. Once I stopped feeling so sad, I started feeling angry. I know now it wasn't your fault, but I was so mad at you for leaving."

"I never would have gone if I'd had any other choice," Luca answers, a note of intense sorrow in his voice. I pause my pig-out session to take his hand and give it a squeeze.

Mr. Lomaglio sighs. "It was never your fault, my son. Sending you away was the most difficult thing we have ever had to do. Like tearing out your heart and sending it on an airplane across the ocean. We never wanted to see you go, Luca."

"Domenica wasn't the only one who cried for you," Mrs. Lomaglio speaks up, those gorgeous green eyes so similar to Luca's shimmering with tears.

"You were born at the wrong time, in the wrong place," her husband continues. "We had no idea that the mafia was closing in on our little neighborhood.

We were not wealthy, and we were not well-known, but we had everything we needed to get by. A house, a garden, and lots of love. We were just happy to have our children—our strong, handsome son, and our sweet, beautiful daughter. If not for the mafia, we would have stayed happy. And we would have stayed together, all in one place, like a family should be."

"We shielded you from those bad men for as long as we could, my love," Luca's mother takes over. "All the years of your childhood, we tried to keep you safe from those who might exploit your strength and bravery, take advantage of your good heart. We wanted you to stay young, carefree, be a child for as long as you could before the world could pick you up and spin you around. But you grew so tall and strong, and the mafia took notice."

"They were always looking for young men to recruit for their grunt work," Mr. Lomaglio says, his face darkening. "Always on the hunt for another good soul to corrupt. They would offer the young boys money, fame, glamorous cars, beautiful women—anything to convince them to join the mafia. Luca, they were circling in on you. We saw them, following you home from school in their big black cars. Watching you play soccer with your friends."

"Do you remember your childhood friend, Alessandro?" Mrs. Lomaglio asks suddenly.

Luca nods. "Yes, of course. We used to climb trees together and go to the park."

"Do you remember when he stopped coming by? When he disappeared?"

Luca looks down at his hands, sadness creeping into his expression.

"Yes."

"They took him. Recruited him right off the street. I can still recall his mother weeping on my shoulder, begging me to help her get him back," she laments. "But there was nothing to be done about it. Once the mafia got its claws on someone, they were forever lost. And after what happened to Alessandro, your father and I had to make a very difficult decision."

"You sent me to live with Uncle Carlo in New York," Luca says softly.

Mr. Lomaglio looks so exhausted. "Yes. We gave you up when you were a teenager. We thought, we hoped, that if you could just stay out of the mafia's reach, they wouldn't be able to catch you. We knew that if you stayed here, they would snatch you up."

"They were threatening us already. Watching our house. Following us to the grocery store. We thought we were giving you a better chance of escaping."

"I know. I don't blame you for what you did," Luca assures them both. "I probably would have done the same thing."

"And then you went away, and I lost my guardian. My playmate," Domenica says, tears tracking down her cheeks. "I missed you so much, Luca. I couldn't understand why you left."

"It was very hard for everyone at first. The house felt so empty without you in it," Mrs. Lomaglio explains, wiping at her eyes. "But we made ourselves go back to our old routines. We had to keep living, because of Domenica."

"And then," Mr. Lomaglio says gravely, "she became so ill. Suddenly. Our joyful little girl was sick all the time, getting weaker by the day. We took her to the doctor again and again, and they could not find out the cause of her illness."

"I don't remember much from those days," Domenica says softly.

"You were fragile. We didn't know what to do. Finally, we got a diagnosis: it was multiple sclerosis. That was devastating to hear. We had already lost our son, and now we were afraid that we might lose our daughter, too," says Mrs. Lomaglio. "We decided that we would do whatever was necessary to help her. No matter the risk."

"The medicine, the equipment, the wheelchair, the private doctors—it was all so expensive. We fought and fought for the government to help us, but it was hard. Nothing was ever enough. One day, things got so bad that I did something I had sworn never to do: I went to the mafia to ask for help," Mr.

Lomaglio admits, and I can tell this is his deepest shame.

"No," Luca breathes.

"Yes. We had to. We needed money, and there was nowhere else to turn. They did help us, once I begged them not to let Domenica fade away. And for a while, everything got a little better. Easier, at least. But then, as we feared, the mafia came to collect their debts," says Luca's mother.

"But we could not pay. The money simply was not there. And so they took what they could from me—my labor. They forced me to do work for them. Grueling, backbreaking work. But that was fine. It was bearable. Until they decided that was not enough. They wanted to make me truly suffer. And so they forced me to be involved in illegal activities. Driving stolen cars. Cleaning crime scenes to throw off the authorities. Working as a guard. I was so exhausted, Luca, between working at the factory, caring for Domenica, and doing this work for the mafia. They were breaking my body, stealing my strength. Finally, they pushed me to take part in the murder of a local baker, an innocent man who refused to pay protection fees to the mafia."

"Papa," Luca says, getting worked up. "Please tell me that isn't true."

Mr. Lomaglio's face is stony, even as the tears fall from his gray eyes.

"I am afraid it is the truth, my son. It is an

atrocity I cannot be forgiven for. They told me if I did not take part, they would kill your mother and Domenica. I could not take the risk. But after it was done, I could no longer look at myself in the mirror. I wanted out, by whatever means necessary. I threatened to go to the police if they did not release me from contract. And by that point, I was already weakened. They had sapped my strength until there was almost nothing left. I was becoming useless to the mafia—more of a liability than an asset."

He pauses and sighs, staring down at the glossy tile floor.

"And so they shifted the debt I owed them. They knew I could never pay them back. I had no money, no power, no strength left in me. But they knew about you. Away in New York, working for your uncle, getting stronger and more impressive every day. They passed the debt from father to son, and suddenly, the terrible fate we worked so hard to keep you from came true. They had found a way to claim you, even after all that time, all that work, all our careful planning."

"And that's why I disappeared, Serena," Luca says, turning to me. "That's why I had to leave when we were teenagers. My life changed. I was no longer living freely." He looks back at his parents, then launches into an explanation of the past decade of his life. He leaves out some of the grittier details, I notice, but he gives them the essentials.

Working for the mafia. Being framed. Prison. Escaping. The explosion. The long road to reunite with me.

"I am so sorry, son," Mr. Lomaglio says, cradling his face in his hands. "I can never forgive myself for what my actions have done to my family."

Luca stands up to walk over and crouch down between his parents' chairs, putting an arm around each of them.

"It isn't your fault. There might have been a time when I blamed you. But not anymore. I know you didn't mean for any of this to happen. It was out of your control, Papa. I don't blame you."

"No," Domenica says suddenly, her pretty face flushed with emotion. "It's my fault. If I hadn't gotten sick, none of that would have happened."

I interject suddenly, "You can't blame yourself. You were just a child, and you didn't choose to fall ill. It's just the way things are sometimes."

Domenica gives me a weak smile.

"Thank you. I feel so guilty when I think about these things. I just wish it had all gone so differently."

"Oh, my sweet sister. If I had known how you were suffering, I would have come back. I would have found a way to help," Luca says sadly.

"Well, now we're all back together," Mrs. Lomaglio says, standing up and putting her hands on her hips. "And I'm going to make the most of it. But for now, I'm sure Serena and Luca would like to rest, after traveling all night to get here."

"That would be wonderful, thank you," I tell her.

"Thank you, Mama," Luca says, kissing her on the cheek.

"I look forward to dinner tonight with my family all together again," Mr. Lomaglio says proudly as his wife leads us out of the room. She takes us out of the main house and across the property to a smaller building, what looks to be a guest house.

"Your father built this by hand," she explains. "We hope that Domenica will live here soon, to give her a little taste of independence before she takes the plunge and moves out on her own. If it were up to me, we could keep her here with us forever, to take care of her. But what she lacks in physical strength, she makes up for in spirit. Your sister is determined to make it on her own and live independently, even in her wheelchair."

"I have no doubt that she will. She's inherited her mother's stubbornness," Luca says, giving his mother a wink and a hug. She laughs.

"Settle in and relax, my loves. Tonight I will make dinner and we can talk some more, but I know you must be so tired," she says.

And with another hug for Luca and for me, she heads back to the main building, leaving Luca and I alone in this adorable, rustic guest house with a gorgeous view of the Apulian hillsides, dotted with olive trees. Luca turns to me and says, "Well, here it is: the place that made me who I am."

"It's just as impressive as you are," I tell him, grinning.

He leans in to kiss me, and instantly any idea of 'relaxing' goes straight out the window.

LUCA

*E*verything about her, the way she feels, smells, looks, it makes my heart warm, and I want the kiss to last forever. For one stupid, boyish moment, I feel like I *can* make it last forever, just me and her, away from everything. But finally, the kiss has to break, and even the sound of our lips moving apart makes my heart beat harder for her.

"No matter what light I see you in," I say, my voice thick and husky, "it always seems to come from inside you."

I watch Serena's soft lips smile slowly, and her eyes rove over my body with hunger in them. In this little room, I can feel that energy building again between us, an energy that neither of us can contain once we realize that we have a moment of privacy together. Even in public, I feel like I can hardly keep my hands off her, but now, there's nothing holding us back.

When she puts her hands on my broad chest and I grip her hips with my powerful, gentle grip, I feel that very feeling welling up inside me. But now, we have a moment to *breathe*. We can enjoy each other's presence, revel in the tense energy between us for a few moments. It's like drinking a fine wine slowly.

I kept the Costa's happy, and no one will ever breathe the location of my family home. Not that many know where that was in the first place. The Cleaners will never find us here, and I feel even safer than being in a safehouse. Here, I can protect all those I love.

But in this beautiful, perfect moment, I'm with my fiancé. Safe. In love.

And with several months to make up for.

I look into her eyes, and I see the beauty written in those nearly glowing irises that grow and shrink to focus on me. The light in the room is dim, but I can see every part of her clearly. It's so familiar, but so new. Her brow, her nose, her cheeks, her chin, her lips, all of her is the most beautiful sight I've ever looked at. I could stay here forever, just gazing at her, feeling like a teenager all over again.

They say you settle down as you get older, but with Serena, I've felt nothing but growing energy, more love for her, and more lust for her body.

"Every day we've been apart, I've wanted to

ravage you," I whisper as her fingers tighten around my shirt, a soft, silent plea for me to take it off. "I've wanted to feel this. To feel you in my hands, *carissima.*"

"I know," she says, her voice a harp's note to my ears. "Luca, I've dreamed about you so many times. I've woken up in the middle of the night so many times thinking you'd be right there beside me." My grip slides around to the small of her back, and I bring her into my embrace as she slides her hands around my torso and rests her head against my chest, listening to the strong, steady sound of my heartbeat.

I rest my chin on her head. "A life without you is not one worth living, Serena," I say. "For that time, I was dead." She looks up at me, and I smile down at her. "But you give me life."

I bring my lips down to hers, and I can feel her sigh with need into the kiss. It starts slow, thoughtful. It's different than it was when we first reunited in that old safehouse, and I let Serena take her time in enjoying my body.

Tonight has meant so much. I feel more filled with love for Serena than ever before, and it's helped to ground us together in something that we can share besides struggle. Struggle has been so much of our relationship. We've fought together. We've run together. We've had to hide together.

So having a moment to step back and enjoy a

moment of reality, a reality that's good and whole...it's a drink of cool water in the desert.

"I want to have more nights like tonight with you, Luca," she says after the kiss breaks and she grinds herself against me, hands roving up and down my body while her front presses into me. Her leg wraps around mine, and her hands go into my back pockets so she can look up at me with lidded eyes. "I want something stable. Family. *Our* family. I want it to grow and be something to be proud of."

"I want to give you all that and more," I say, "and I want every night filled with *this*."

I walk her back to the bed, and she climbs back onto it, sitting on folded legs and looking up at me. She reaches up and gives my shirt a tug, and I smile. The fact that she gets so much pleasure out of my body never stops giving me pride. It's all the more motivation to keep my body as fit as I can, even when all this rough and tumble living settles down. I want to make myself perfect for those soft eyes every day.

She sits there like an angel, a single lamp's light behind her lighting the room, making her look like a true angel with a crown of golden hair spilling down her shoulders. In contrast, I loom over her with my broad shoulders and imposing, dark form, like a shadow.

I reach down to my shirt and pull it up over my body, drawing the move out slowly so she can take in every inch of my torso, every ripple, every muscle. She puts her slender hands to my stomach and brings her face to it to kiss it softly, nearly worshipping my body. Her hands run up my sides, and she turns her face to let her cheek rub up against my abs, feeling their warmth, nails tracing along my sides.

"Let me taste you," she begs me in a pleading tone I can't resist, "there's so much of you I want to feel inside me again."

"You can have it," I say, reaching down and running my hand through her golden hair, feeling how soft and thick her locks are, resisting the urge to take a fistful of it tight and fuck her senseless right then and there without hesitation, without restraint. "But I want to *see* you first."

She starts to take her shirt off hurriedly, but I kneel down onto the bed with her to stop her. My hands push hers aside, and I take hold of the soft fabric to lift it off. I let my warm hands brush against her skin as they go, and we move as if we're in a dream together, exploring each other's bodies like we have all the time in the world.

Because for just one night, we do.

I push her to her back after I've lifted the shirt off her, exposing that unbelievable body of hers, and I bend over her to start kissing her. I kiss her from her waist to her belly, then up to her breasts, still covered by her bra.

I let my hands grope them through the thick

fabric, but it isn't long before I can't take it anymore. While I lean forward and tickle her neck with kisses, my hands reach behind her and unhook the thing and pull it off her. When I'm getting too excited and I'm starting to bite at her neck, I push myself up to loom over her exposed form, drinking her with my eyes.

I hadn't noticed it before, but her breasts have started to swell from her pregnancy. That, or they're fuller and more ripe than ever before, and my cock swells tight in my pants.

I bring my mouth down to her nipples and let my breath wash over them. The sound of her excited gasp is music to my ears. I breathe on the other, holding my mouth so perilously close to her, teasing her painfully. She arches her back to push herself up to me, but I don't let her reach—I keep myself just out of reach, my hot breath the only thing stimulating those sensitive nipples.

They're stiff and begging to be toyed with, though, and soon, I give into the urge to devour them. I descend, first letting my tongue flick them while my hands grip her hips, holding her under my control as she lets out a desperate gasp. I take one of the swollen nubs between my teeth, letting the hard edges tease it harder and needier. She starts to pump her hips gently, hands scrambling for anywhere to hold onto, and I can swear she's about to come right then, her pants still on.

I let my tongue taste the soft skin of her breasts until I'm ready to reward her for her patience. I trail down her belly again, gently caressing her before I get to the button of her pants. With my teeth, I pop it open and grip the waist of her pants. She wiggles in a desperate effort to get out of them and help me pull them down, panties and all.

The sight of her hips stirs that animalistic energy within me. Their curve, the tone of her skin, that beautiful sanctuary where her legs meet, it's enough to drive me wild. But I know she's desperate to taste me as I am for her, and I won't deny my princess anything.

I stand up and look down at her as she squirms on the bed completely naked, her olive skin beyond beautiful on the sheets in the dim light.

Once I'm up, her eyes flutter open, and she looks at me with anticipation, biting her lip as I open my own pants and slide them off. Normally, I'd just let the monstrous shaft of my cock spring free alone, but I want her to see every inch of my body in the same way I see hers. Nothing between us, nothing hiding from each other.

I want Serena, and Serena wants me.

So I kick my denim pants off my legs, revealing my pillar-like, muscular legs, and she crawls forward on the bed to my stiff, bulging cock. It's standing straight upright, extended toward her like a spear that she wraps her hand around, looking hungrily at the tip.

Her other hand goes to my balls, feeling their weight, holding them in her palm, letting out a soft sigh at how heavy and full of need they are.

She works her hands up and down my shaft slowly, and it's like an engine rumbling to life within me. I tilt my head back, closing my eyes and shutting out everything else but her touch. It's that much more intense of a feeling when I feel her tongue taste the tip of my dark, bulging crown.

Her hand slides up and down my shaft while her mouth plays with my crown. She runs her tongue around and over the tip, making my balls tense and my whole body feel warm. I reach forward and caress her hair in my hands, stroking it almost in a steady rhythm as she tastes me.

"I've missed this so much," she breathes over my manhood, and I can feel the desire to let loose and go wild in her every touch. She wants to work me until I release myself onto her, and it takes enormous willpower not to encourage her to do just that right now.

A few minutes more of this, though, and I don't know if I'll be so willing to hold back.

Finally, I feel her warm, soft lips kiss the tip of my cock while her hands lavish the shaft with attention. I hear her moaning softly into it as her lips part and she flicks the tip with her tongue. She takes the crown into her mouth and starts running the very tip of her tongue around the edges of my swollen crown. Even though it's my most sensitive part of my body, my cock is tough, and the faster the motions of her hand get, the more her teeth graze my tip, the more it excites me. I feel like my body's tension is unlocking itself bit by bit, and it's wild to me that this tiny woman in front of me can have such an effect on my massive body.

She starts to lick the bottom of my crown on the underside of my cock, right where it meets the beginning of my shaft. I smile as I realize she's been learning from how I tease her when my tongue is deep in her pussy, trailing up until it can toy with her clit.

I've taught this woman terrible things, and I'll teach her more and more, if I have my way.

Her tongue gets more adventurous, and she starts taking more of my shaft into her mouth, making sure to wrap her lips around my whole cock. It's not easy to take everything into her mouth, but the more of my cock's weight she feels resting on her tongue, the more she desires me. The more she wants to take in. The more she's willing to try.

"Your eyes are bigger than your mouth, Serena," I chuckle before a quick jolt of heat rushes up my cock. Serena answers me with a hungry sigh. She's not going to be turned away that easily.

She starts moving her tongue like a ripple,

putting pressure as far back down my cock as she can reach and slowly dragging it up the underside of my cock. My crown is at the back of her mouth, kissing the soft, hot roof of her mouth so far back. With her free hand, Serena massages my balls, and I know she's coaxing me, begging me, desperately wanting to taste me.

I often take my cock out of her mouth at this point and thrust it deep into her pussy to finish. But tonight, Serena is working hard, and the hot feeling running through my whole body tells me it's paying off. I'll make it pay off for her.

Hell, I'll give her that and so, so much more.

I let myself lose my concentration and look down at Serena. The mere sight of her is enough to push me over the edge. Her golden hair sits beautifully on her shoulders, getting messy as she relentlessly worships my cock. Her eyes aren't closed—she's looking up at me, love in her eyes as she sucks my dark pillar. This is the love of my life, the most beautiful woman I've ever laid eyes on...and she's getting as much out of this as I am.

Soon, her free hand leaves my balls and slides down to her legs, where she starts to run it up and down her lower lips, and her eyes close again. Her lips tighten, and she gives a soft little yelp into my cock. I can hear the wet sound of her touching herself, and knowing that being on her knees at my cock has put her in this dizzy, lustful state makes me release.

My balls tighten, and my cock gets tenser than ever. Serena can tell what's happening, and she gets a firm grip on me for fear that I should pull away. I could give her hair a squeeze to make her back off and let me ruin her face, her perfect body, all with my seed, but I want her to follow through with what she's gotten herself into.

White-hot bliss wells up inside me, a tension that's almost painful and swelling with every half-second. Finally, my mouth hangs open, and I release a shot of hot seed into Serena's mouth, and the groan I let out is almost in harmony with the sigh of delight she gasps. My cock throbs, releasing more of me into her, but Serena doesn't pull herself away, nor does she let up—her hands keep working my shaft while she keeps my crown in her lips, taking in every bit of me I have to give.

She sighs in deep, blissful satisfaction as my cock throbs, and she runs her tongue up my shaft one last time before taking her lips from me. As she lets her fingers play up my cock one last time, a final spurt of my seed empties itself onto her chest, and she sits back, letting her head fall back while she props herself up on her elbows and smiling contentedly.

She's proud of herself.

I feel heat glowing around me as I breathe

raggedly. My knees are weak, but not so weak that I can't give her what she's got coming next.

"You're smug," I say with a smile, kneeling over her and massaging my cock with my own hand.

"Maybe a little," she says with a wink. "I missed...everything about that."

I grab her hips and push her forward while I crawl onto the bed, and she gasps as I put my hands on her sensitive inner thighs. I grip her carefully, brushing the flesh with my thumbs while gazing down at her.

"Enjoy it while it lasts," I growl, and she starts to breathe a little faster as I part her legs. "Because if you think I'm done with you, you've got another thing coming."

With that, I bring my face down to her pussy and breathe in the scent, and I feel my cock twitch again, despite having just released itself. Serena is enough to get me going all over again in hardly any time at all.

I let my tongue out, and licks the honey off Serena's lips. It's the same sweet taste as I remember, made all the sweeter for how long I've been away from her, away from her honey. The strongest liquor in the world can't compare to her and what she does to me.

My tongue tastes her again, and again going deeper each time, and each swipe earns a gasp from Serena—her hands push into my hair and grip my head, her hips thrust up into my face, and she throws her head back.

Tasting me has made her so ready, so needy, that she's already gotten my face doused in her wetness. My hands take hold of her hips and keep them down while I go to work on her poor lips. I kiss her, pressing my lips to her pussy while my tongue ventures deep into her, drawing up more honey that she pours out for me and using it to torment her clit with each stroke.

The taste makes my whole mouth water for more. Between the come on her chest and her come on my face, we're a mess, and the room feels hot, but we're lost in each other. Dizzy, drunk, whatever you want to call it, we can't keep ourselves off one another any longer. My hands take in every curve of her hips and her legs while I feast on her.

She squirms under me, desperately trying to move around and thrust harder as if that would help her finish any faster, but I control the situation perfectly. My grip on her is tight, and I show her that she's mine by keeping her down on the bed, subjecting her to my mouth on her pussy. I can feel her starting to tighten already, her pussy starting to wetten further and further in anticipation.

My rhythm gets steady. I dart out to her clit, stroke, and retreat, then over again, teasing her on her clit for just a split second before leaving her, and soon, that builds up little by little until she thrusts her hips up harder than ever before, and I release her to hold her up by her ass.

She lets out a silent scream of pleasure, holding my hair tight as she comes, and I bury my mouth and my face in her folds while they pulse and tighten around me, her whole body coming beautifully in my hands and all over my face.

"Oh Luca!" she breathes out, panting with desire, but I don't respond. Instead, I start stroking her again as if I'd never stopped.

I go faster this time, sometimes deeper, exploring more of her that I'd dreamt of so many nights while wishing I was at her side, protecting her. I keep going until I feel that tension building up again, and I follow it through to release. With one orgasm having come through in careless bliss, more come more easily, and I drive them all with my tongue until I can hardly feel my face.

My mouth works her so long that I'm stiff and ready again.

Even though I've lost track of the orgasms wracking her body, I hear her give a whimper of complaint when I take my face from her lips and crawl up her body to pin her down by the wrists. Just as she opens her mouth to protest, I silence her with a wet, hot kiss at the same time that I drive my cock into her pussy.

She sucks in a breath when I enter her, and we kiss sloppily while I start bucking into her. We're both so overwhelmed with stimulation that we can hardly tell up from down anymore. All I know is that my hard cock is inside her pussy where it feels best, and her hot insides are wet and welcoming to me.

Our bodies pressed up against each other, I pick up a steady rhythm, ramming into her and grinding up against every spot I know to drive her wild. I pull back to loom over her, and my hands go to her breasts, thumbs toying with those nipples I bit at when we first got started. That feels like ages ago, we've gotten so lost in the moment, and my heart pounds furiously.

She looks up at me like she can't believe how soon I'm ready for her again, and the mix of excitement and worry on her face tells me everything I need to give her another night she'll never forget. I hold nothing back, savoring the feeling of her breasts while I take her, freely letting my own pleasure roil up into an unstoppable wave that soon starts shaking me from the groin up to my chest.

"Serena," I moan, and I try to bring more words to my mouth, but my mind is just a mess of lust and desire, and that's all I can say, over and over again until I feel my balls start to grow tight again.

I pour myself into her, letting out a ragged groan with my second orgasm as my whole body shudders. I've been through fights that put my life at risk, but nothing is as intense and fierce a rush as coming into my woman.

I hear her delighted sigh through the haze of my orgasm, and finally, still hard inside her, I feel the last of my seed emptying into her.

Slowly, gently, I lower myself to her, and we stare into each other's eyes for a few moments. Finally, I pull out of her slowly, slow enough that it doesn't hurt her, and I turn her so that she can spoon into me comfortably.

I slip my hand between her legs and massage her, feeling her whole body tingle while I gently bring her down from the rush, and I kiss her neck.

"I meant what I said," I whisper into her ear as I feel her breathing slowly, glowing.

"Meant what?"

"I want to give you nights like this every day," I say, my voice deep and rough. "And I'll stop at nothing to make that happen."

While I feel Serena wiggling into me and getting ready to doze off into sleep, messy and hot as we are, I know my words to be a truer desire than anything I've felt in my life.

The only question is just how much will get in our way.

"You look beautiful," Luca assures me for probably the hundredth time this morning. I'm standing in the middle of the tiny combined kitchen and living room space of the guest house, looking down worriedly at my outfit. It's just starting to get hot here in Italy, and considering I arrived here at the Lomaglio residence wearing my filthy sweatshirt and jeans, it was high time for a change of wardrobe. Unfortunately, I can't even dream of fitting into Mrs. Lomaglio's clothing —she is both much shorter and considerably rounder than I am. So Domenica, being the ever-helpful and generous girl she is, offered me some of her clothes for now, until I have time to pick out some new stuff for myself.

But Domenica is a seventeen-year-old girl who is very, very slender and not at all pregnant, so her clothing is a little bit tight and youthful for my body. I'm currently wearing one of her dresses, a knee-length blue frock with white flowers and spaghetti straps, along with a pair of Mrs. Lomaglio's sandals. Everything fits to some degree, but I still feel pretty weird. It's strange, you'd think after wearing a ton of hand-me-down donated clothes at the women's shelter, this would be second nature. But somehow, it's weirder when you know the people whose clothing it is. Or maybe it's just weird because I only barely know them. We just met, and now I'm living in their guest house and wearing their clothes.

Oh, and I'm pregnant with their long-lost son's baby.

Just a recipe for awkwardness, all around. But in their defense, the Lomaglios have been overwhelmingly kind and generous, constantly offering me more food, more drinks, asking if I'm comfortable, if there's anything else I need. It's very, very nice of them, but after spending so much time with my own uptight, closed-off mother for so long, it's a shock to my system to spend time with such a warm, loving family. It's not that my own mother doesn't love me, of course, she just has a very different way of showing it—and by that I mean she rarely shows it at all.

Luca's family, on the other hand, is almost over the top. They hug each other, they touch each other's faces, they profess their love like it's the most natural thing in the world. It's something I never would have pictured for Luca when I first met him. He seemed so tough and cool. *Too* cool to have come from such a cuddly family. But the more I get to know him, the clearer it is to me that this is how he grew up. He may be a powerful, imposing, even dangerous man, but underneath that jagged exterior, love and loyalty come before all else.

"I'm not sure my boobs quite fit in this dress," I mutter, looking down at my unusually impressive cleavage in this tiny dress. Luca walks over and puts his arms around me, smiling.

"Looks pretty good to me," he remarks cheekily.

I roll my eyes. "Well, of course you'd say that. I just don't want to look scandalous. Especially not with your family around. I'm trying to make a good impression here."

"Oh, don't worry about that. They already love you," he says, kissing me on the cheek. "Now, come on. I want to get to Alberobello before the gelato stands start closing for the afternoon. Don't you?"

"Oh yes, please," I laugh, letting him sweep me away out into the Italian sunshine. His father is away at work—he has a job in an office nowadays. Mrs. Lomaglio is busy cleaning, cooking, and fussing over Domenica, as usual, and Domenica is wrapped up in studying for her online classes. This leaves Luca and I all day to ourselves to explore and relax, finally spend some quality time together. We climb into the car and ride off through the rolling golden hills, holding hands over the center console.

The scenery outside is absolutely stunning. I can see why Luca remembers this place so fondly. It looks like a postcard, but not exactly the kind of landscape I would normally think of when someone brings up Italy.

It's less green than Tuscany, less mountainous than the northern regions. But it has its own wild, humble beauty. Birds flutter from one massive clump of thorny underbrush to the next, chirping and singing. Golden-greenish fields full of brown-and-white cows. Endless blue skies without a cloud in sight. Piled stone walls about knee-height frame the roads on either side.

I can perfectly imagine young Luca running free in these fields, climbing trees, kicking a soccer ball around, getting into trouble. The thought makes me smile.

It's a lovely drive out to the little town of Alberobello, which first appears on the horizon as a pearly-white spot in the distance beneath an incredibly lush blue sky.

Luca explains that this little town is home to several examples of historical architecture called *trulli* like what we saw when we were escaping in our latest high speed chase.

Once we park and start walking around, I can see why he brought me here. The houses are bright white, made of rock and built straight into the lime-stone, with cone-shaped gray roofs. The streets are lined with them, and many of the *trulli* have been transformed into little pottery shops and art galleries, while other buildings are still in use as residences.

Colorful shelves jut out from beneath round windows, holding pots of flowers, number plaques, sometimes surnames. Tourists are around every corner, professional photographers traveling from all over the world to snap photos of the interesting architecture and gorgeous colors. It's nice to be able to enjoy the interesting architecture, this time around.

As we wander down the tiny cobblestone streets, Luca turns to me with a grin.

"What do you think?" he asks, as if there's any other answer to give.

"It's amazing," I tell him, shaking my head in awe. "I've never seen anything like this."

"Crazy to think I grew up just down the road from this."

"Yeah! When I think about where I grew up, this seems like some kind of fantasy land."

"New York has its charms, too. There are certainly much worse places to live," he says, shrugging. "But for me, this will always be home."

"I'm happy that you grew up somewhere like this. Everything you've seen, everything you've been through—all of that has made you into the amazing man you are today," I say, kissing the back of his hand.

"Come on, you sweet, sentimental woman, let's get you some gelato," he says.

We head down the street to a village square which looks to be meticulously maintained, full of tourists oohing and ahhing over the picturesque surroundings. We sit down at a little cafe, taking an outdoors table so we can people-watch and enjoy the sunshine.

Luca gets pistachio ice cream and I get hazelnut, and after that we order coffee and pastries. We sit there, just talking and soaking up the sun, being lazy and happy together, for what must be hours.

Finally, when the little woman running the cafe comes out to gently warn us that they're closing up shop soon, we thank her and head back to the car.

We take our time driving back to the Lomaglio property, stopping on the side of the road to explore an open field, to snap a picture together in front of an especially photogenic olive tree. We're acting like embarrassing, goofy tourists in love, even though Luca knows this place by heart, and it's wonderful.

By the time we make it back home, we're both sunkissed and tired and unable to stop smiling.

I don't know what the future holds for us, and I know this lovely dream has to end at some point, but for now, I'm just drinking in every last drop of happiness I can get. Luca is alive, he's in my arms, and I can't imagine anything better than this.

We wash up and get changed for dinner, heading over to the main house. As soon as we step through the door, we're greeted by the smells of delicious cheeses, meats, fish, and pasta Luca's mother has been preparing all day.

I have to wonder if she really goes all out like this every evening, or if she's just amping up the menu because Luca is here. Either way, I am sure as hell not going to complain. Especially since I'm eating for two.

At the dinner table, we tell Luca's family about the amazing day we've had, and I gush about how beautiful the countryside is, how friendly all the people are—including them.

I'm feeling so relaxed that I even let Domenica pour me the tiniest glass of red wine, which I sip contentedly. I've never been a huge drinker, but being pregnant, I've really missed having some wine or a cocktail every now and then.

And of course, since they're Italian, they know exactly what wine to pair with what kind of meal. If there's one thing I have learned from my brief time here in Italy, it's that even when money is tight, Italians don't skimp on the quality of their diet.

They might skip buying a new dress or a new car, but they always eat like kings.

And I can *certainly* appreciate that.

As I'm digging into a plate of pasta, the family starts sharing stories about what Luca was like as a young boy. Apparently, he got into trouble in school —a lot. Not for anything too criminal, but he was very energetic and prone to pranking people.

"One time, he put a cricket in his teacher's purse," Mrs. Lomaglio says, clucking her tongue. "The poor woman almost had a heart attack right there in the middle of class."

"Oh, that's awful," I laugh, playfully hitting Luca on the arm. He shrugs, looking a little sheepish as he reaches for another scoop of pasta.

"*She* was awful. She used to make me write with my right hand even though I'm left-handed. Anytime I would go back to using my left hand, she would slap my wrist with a ruler!" he says defensively. "She was my least favorite teacher."

"Oh, was that Maestra Mancini?" Domenica asks, wrinkling her nose.

"Yes!" Luca exclaims. "Don't tell me you had to deal with her, too. How old is that woman? Is she still teaching?"

"Ugh, she was my least favorite teacher, too. And yes, she's probably still teaching now. I don't think that woman will ever die. She's immortal," Domenica giggles.

"That's not nice," her mother scolds, though I can tell she's fighting a smile.

"Luca was such a troublemaker. So much energy.

Always falling out of trees and catching little animals. Do you remember when you brought home that turtle?" Mr. Lomaglio says.

Luca chuckles. "Yeah, of course. I loved that little guy."

"What was his name again?" his mother asks.

"Baffo," Luca answers, laughing. "I kept him in a cardboard box with plants I picked inside it. I had the hardest time trying to figure out what to feed him without asking you and having you find out I was hiding a turtle in my room."

"I don't remember that," Domenica says, frowning.

"You were just a baby back then," Luca says. "I think that might have been why I thought I could get away with it—Mama and Papa were too busy taking care of you to notice me sneaking food out of the pantry to feed to Baffo."

"Oh, but I did find him," Mrs. Lomaglio says, rolling her eyes. "By accident. I was cleaning your room one day, looking for your soccer jersey while you were at school, when I tripped over that cardboard box and out came Baffo. I screamed so loud the neighbors called the police, remember?"

"They called me, too. They thought someone had broken into the house," Mr. Lomaglio says, shaking his head and grinning. "I rushed home from work only to find my wife, baby, two policemen, and a turtle in my living room. I have never been so relieved and confused in my life."

"Oh, I bet you were in big trouble when you got home from school," I remark to Luca.

"I don't think I was allowed to play outside for a week," he says.

"Served you right for scaring me so much," his mother chuckles.

"I think Baffo was probably much happier as a free turtle than living in a cardboard box in my bedroom, anyway," Luca admits, grinning.

"Oh!" I exclaim suddenly, putting my hands on my stomach. There's a weird sensation in my belly, something bigger than just butterflies, bigger than just nausea. I look over at Luca, who's looking at me with concern. A smile jumps to my face. "I think the baby just kicked!"

Mrs. Lomaglio gasps and comes rushing over, with her husband and daughter trailing after her, all of them eager to put their hands on my stomach in case it happens again.

"Maybe it's a sign that the baby wants to be called Baffo," Domenica giggles.

"I don't think that's on our shortlist of names," Luca says, laughing.

We wait quietly, patiently for a few minutes. Every one of them has a hand on my barely-protruding stomach. At first, I think it might have been a fluke, just indigestion or something. But then

—it happens again! Everyone gasps, and Mrs. Lomaglio almost starts to cry with happiness.

"This is a cause for celebration!" she declares, rushing off to the kitchen and emerging again with a plate of sweet pastries.

I have no idea how this woman cooks and bakes so much all the time. She's like a machine. But we all gladly partake of the sweets, gushing to each other about how excited we are for the baby.

I know it will be awhile, but I'm already so excited to meet this kid, no matter how crazy the world around us may be.

After dinner, we help Mrs. Lomaglio tidy up, and then head off to bed. I fall asleep smiling, lying next to the man I love, the man I thought I lost, who came back to me by a miracle.

I dream the same dreams I've been having for the past few months—Luca, the baby, and me, living happily together in a cozy house. Just doing the dishes together, cooking dinner together, spending time in each other's company like we should be.

And when I wake up early the next morning, I trot out to the porch to watch the bees and butter-flies flitting around in the garden. The plants are all growing high and healthy, ready for the harvest. It's a modest life the Lomaglios lead out here, but they're comfortable. They're happy.

They don't have much beyond the necessities, but they eat well, they're as healthy as can be considering the parents' ages and Domenica's illness. They love each other unabashedly, and they spend their days in quiet joy, especially now that Luca is here.

I can't help but think about how much I envy them. This simple, humble, beautiful life they lead out here in the Apulian countryside—it's like a dream.

I imagine what it would be like for Luca and I to live this way. To find a little house of our own in the golden hills, plant a garden, grow some of our own food and go to the farmer's market or the grocery store for the rest. Eat wholesome, delicious, lovingly-cooked food. Watch the sunrises and sunsets together. Drink wine. Eat cheese and fruit. Drive down the winding roads and find new places to kiss each other under the bright blue sky.

It's everything I never knew I wanted. Maybe it's not the most exciting way to live, but when I really think about it, I've probably had enough excitement to last me a lifetime.

I just want to be comfortable and happy and surrounded by love—and I can't imagine a better place for our little baby to grow up. Especially with Luca's family so close by. It just seems perfect.

After the sun rises, Luca joins me on the porch, kissing me on the cheek and wishing me a good morning. I'm just about to tell him about my dream, about how wonderful it would be to stay here and build a life together—when my phone suddenly buzzes in my lap. I pick it up and read the text message I've just received.

And immediately, an alarm bell starts sounding off in my head.

Something is wrong. Very, very wrong.

"**W**hat's the matter?" I ask, stepping forward to her, reading the concern and confusion written on her face. "Did you get some news from back home?"

"I...I don't know," she says, glancing up at me. "It's a message from my mom. But it's just an X." She shakes her head, forcing a smile. "Never mind. It was probably just an accident. I'm jumping at shadows. It's just kind of weird to hear from her. Feels like we're in a whole different world all the way out here, and the past few weeks have been so crazy that it feels a lot longer than it has been."

I'm not entirely convinced that's all that bothers Serena, but I don't want to push her, so with a raised eyebrow I nod, then soften my expression into a smile and come to give her a hug as she puts her phone away.

"That's understandable. You've been through a lot. Give it some time, and everything will settle down in your mind—a clear head is important in times like this."

She nods, taking those words to reassure herself as much as I try to reassure her. "Right." Brushing a strand of hair out of her face, she flutters her eyes up at me. "So, what's the plan for today?"

"Besides the massive breakfast that's about to start smelling heavenly inside?" I say, nodding back to the house, where I can see the silhouettes of my parents through the reflective glass moving around in the kitchen.

"Right, assuming I survive another feast," she says with a laugh, and I help her up to her feet, even though she doesn't need it.

"I convinced them to hold back from cooking dinner for us again so we could get out for a little time to ourselves," I say, holding her around the waist and beaming down at her. "I found out that an old friend of mine opened a restaurant in town, so we need to get down there and see whether it's bad enough that I can give him a hard time."

"*Don't!*" she laughs, slapping me on the chest before I scoop her into a hug, chuckling and peppering her cheek with kisses. "Seriously, be nice! Let's not accidentally make any rivals while we're here."

"I'm kidding—he was this big musclebound oaf

back in the day, so it's funny to see him running a little restaurant now. But he's a good man," I say, giving her a light squeeze.

"Sounds like you," she says with a teasing quirk of an eyebrow.

"Exactly, which is why I'm sure it will be the best pasta you've ever had. But that doesn't mean I won't make fun of him while I have the chance."

~

Later that day, my old friend doesn't prove me wrong.

The little restaurant he inherited from his father is on a plaza in one of the villages nearby, and it's a cozy hole in the wall that tourists usually wouldn't notice unless they knew what to look for. There are about ten tables in the place—not too shabby for this area. The floors are old, dark wood, and there are pictures from local history and important people all around the walls, along with a fireplace toward the back.

"This place is cozy," Serena remarks as we sit at one of the little tables, watching a few more people trickle in for dinnertime. It's a mix of younger people like us on romantic dates and older couples who are probably regulars or friends of the family— that's how places like this stay open.

"The family always did have an eye for interior

design, as much as you can call it that around here," I say, beaming around the place.

She casts a look toward the kitchen, then whispers to me, "You don't think we're crowding the place, do you?" She tears off a piece of the tough bread that's been laid in front of us. "We ordered our food more than half an hour ago."

"That's normal, I promise," I say after taking a drink of the soda in front of me. If Serena isn't drinking, I'd rather not either, despite my friend's insistence that he give us a bottle of some of his oldest wine. "Service times in Italy are nothing like they are back in the USA. It's something you just...get used to. Kind of like how lunch and dinner can be all-day events, you usually go to a restaurant expecting to just sit around and talk for a long time before anything else happens."

She looks thoughtful for a few moments, then nods slowly. "Okay, I get it. I don't know if I like it yet, but I get it," she adds with a playful smile, and I grin, crossing my legs with hers under the table.

"I think it's more relaxed," I say with a shrug of my shoulders. "I always felt rushed in places in America, but you know, the country's changing. Who knows what it'll be like a few years from now."

"Maybe more than that, down here," she points out.

I nod, looking around at the old building. "A great deal more than that, true."

Before much longer, though, our food arrives, and we start eating—and I'm proud to see that my friend hasn't made a liar of me. Serena eats the food ravenously, giving me a thumbs-up between mouthfuls of pasta.

She's having *orecchiette alle cime di rapa*, to be precise. It's a traditional southern dish made with pan-fried broccoli, anchovies, chili, and garlic. A little unusual for the American tastes, but Serena seems to be appreciating it without hesitation.

It makes me happy to see her taken care of like this. I worry sometimes that all the stress of running around so much will wear on her, but she seems to have more energy than ever. And as my old friend cleans the bar up at the counter, he gives me a knowing grin with a glance to Serena when she's not looking.

I smirk and wave him off, and Serena looks up at me, wiping her mouth with her napkin.

"What?"

"Nothing," I say with a chuckle, "just old friends teasing me." I give her a once-over and add, "You make a good impression around here."

That makes her blush, and she shoves more food into her mouth to avoid acknowledging the fact that she's the most beautiful woman in the whole village.

But as the dinner goes on and we get closer to the end of our plates, Serena takes her phone out and sets it on the side of the table, periodically checking it.

I ignore it at first, but once it's out and on the table, I notice that Serena's demeanor seems to have taken an anxious turn. In fact, she's seemed a little tense all day—the easy going, loving energy between us so far has seemed muted ever since she got that message in the morning.

"You're looking at the message again, aren't you?" I say as I finish my dinner, setting my fork down and crossing my arms to rest on the table.

"Sorry, I know it's rude, I-"

I wave it off, shaking my head. "Oh come on, I don't care about that, Serena—I can tell something's bothering you. Did your mother have bad news to give you? Is she okay?"

She looks up at me with a little relief, as though she's glad to know that I'm only worried about her wellbeing first and foremost. Done with her food, she pushes it aside while I scoot my chair to sit beside her and look at the message she shows me.

"Here, look at this." She holds out her phone to me, and I take the little thing in my hand. She has an app pulled up—a secure, encrypted messaging app that makes it difficult to trace without the kind of resources only a government agency might have.

The little glowing screen displays a message that looks like it's from Serena's mother Luisa. But it's nothing. It's just one, simple little letter. An X. Probably accidentally hit it while she was getting dressed or something.

"Am I missing something?" I ask, handing the phone back to her. "I don't understand, it looks like an accidental text from Luisa."

Serena looks at me with increasingly worried eyes. "Mom outright *refuses* to use texting, she always has. She's like, you know, old-fashioned. She's always just called me and kept me talking for an hour or even hand-written a letter. The few times I've ever gotten a text from her, it's just been something quick like 'call me.' I've been trying to get her to get better at texting for years, but she never budges."

I furrow my brow. Any other time, I wouldn't worry about something like this, but now of all times, I have to admit that just about anything could make me suspicious.

"Then why just an X? Why not send you just a normal greeting?" I ask, crossing my arms.

Serena shakes her head, still looking at the screen. "No... It's that... When I was younger, and I first got a cellphone, she hated the idea. She thought I was going to spend all my days on it and get bad self-esteem. The only reason she let me get it, is in case of emergencies. I guess because of dad's job. So when we agreed to get a family package, she made me promise to text her with one letter if I was in trouble." She trails off, looking to me with worried eyes.

I frown, rubbing my chin with a hand for a moment before I reply.

"An X," I guess, and Serena nods.

"But that was for you texting her, and that was a long time ago. Do you really think it's not just coincidence?"

Serena frowns, looking at the phone again.

"I want to think it's a coincidence, but she hasn't gotten back to me since. Do you think this is her secret SOS?"

"Luisa isn't totally in the dark. Through some of my friends back home, I had her updated on some very basic details about what's going on—she knows she can't reach you by letter-mail right now or make international calls." I smile warmly and add, "We have eyes on her, too, remember. She's probably safe and sound, and like you said, probably got frustrated trying to type up a text."

"True, that's possible," she admits, not looking totally convinced. "But that still doesn't explain why she hasn't gotten back to me. Gosh, that sounds overly paranoid, doesn't it?" She leans an elbow on the table, resting her head on her hand and rubbing her forehead.

"Not at all," I assure her, giving her shoulder a squeeze and massaging her neck with one hand a little. "You have every right to be worried for your mother. This is why we take precautions. Tomorrow,

I'll get in touch with my men and have someone check up on her to make sure everything is okay."

She smiles at me, looking appreciative. "I'd like that. Thanks, Luca." She looks back down to the phone, pursing her lips a little. "I'll just try texting her again, and let her know that I am going to die in pasta heaven.

"*Bene*," I say and wave down the server to beckon them over to us. "In the meantime, though, don't think you're getting out of here without dessert," I say, a smile on my face, but when I look back to Serena, I see her looking at her phone with worry.

I listen to my lover when I see that kind of worry on her face.

And whatever the real situation is with that message from her mother, I don't have a good feeling about it.

"Oh god, I'm stuffed," I groan, sitting back in the chair. Across the table, Luca laughs, setting his fork down and taking a sip of his red wine.

"I'm a little jealous," he says, looking back to me and grinning. "I wish I had the excuse to eat for two."

I pat my belly. "Well, don't be too jealous. I think the whole getting-to-eat-a-lot thing is really only a fair trade-off for the constant exhaustion and nausea."

"How has that been lately, by the way?" he asks, leaning forward and furrowing his brow. I love the way he does this—effortlessly transitions from goofing around to taking me very seriously. I can tell that underneath his jokes, he's often worried about me. Worried about the baby.

He keeps his concerns to himself most of the

time, probably because he doesn't want to give me anything else to fret about, but I know him better than anyone. I can see when something is bothering him.

I can feel it.

"Much better, actually. I think being around your family and… well, you, has helped a lot with the sickness," I assure him, reaching across to take his hand.

He nods slowly, and I can see the cogs turning in his mind.

"I'm sorry, Serena," he says suddenly, his face going solemn, his voice lowering.

I tilt my head to one side, confused at this sudden apology.

"Sorry? For what?"

He looks back up at me, those bright green eyes full of feeling.

"It's my fault. How rough the past few months have been for you. I should have been here, by your side, helping you all along. I feel like I abandoned you at the worst possible time. You're carrying my baby—our baby—and for all that time you had to do it alone. I can't help but think that's the reason you were so sick. You were stressed out and scared and lonely, just like anyone would be in that situation. I should have been there, Serena. I'm so sorry."

I give him a smile, shaking my head.

"Luca, I don't blame you for anything. You know that, right? None of this is your fault."

"If you hadn't met me, gotten tangled up in this mess—"

"Then I wouldn't be carrying this baby," I interject. "I wouldn't be in love with the most amazing man in the world. I wouldn't be here right now, sitting in a genuine Italian restaurant eating genuine Italian pasta and drinking a very small, very cautious glass of red wine."

I shrug and squeeze his hand.

"Luca. You have to understand: I don't regret anything. I don't regret any single thing of what has happened since you came back into my life that day at Bathing Beauty. Hell yeah, it's been difficult. Of course, it has. But it's worth it. Everything—every hardship, every moment of fear, every misstep, it's led me here. With you. And I can't think of anywhere else I would rather be right now."

He stands up and walks over to help me up, kissing my hand like a true gentleman. Gazing into my eyes with pure devotion, he says, "I've never met anyone quite like you. So strong. So brave. Our child is lucky to have you as a mother. And I am lucky to call you my fiancée."

We pay the bill and stroll back out onto the cobblestone streets of this quaint little countryside village. The sun is setting over the golden hills, casting pink and orange streaks through the sky.

There's a pleasant breeze keeping us from getting too hot in the balmy, early summer evening.

Hand in hand, we walk down the street toward the sound of live music playing, both of us wondering what the commotion is all about. We turn a corner into a village square ringed with vendors selling gelato, wine, spritzers, *sgagliozze*, and *cannoli*. There's a band of lively musicians playing folk music while in the center of the square, a big gathering of people are dancing, some in couples, others in groups of young women.

There are many more people sitting at little tables arranged on the perimeter, watching the dance while they sip wine and chat. It's an almost magical scene: the music, the laughter, the smells of salt and sweetness mingling in the air.

Luca turns to me with an adventurous, mischievous look on his handsome face.

"What?" I ask warily. He grins and pulls me along behind him as we join the dancers. "Oh no, Luca, I'm not much of a dancer!"

"Don't worry," he says, grinning, "I am."

He takes the lead, spinning me around through the village square, teaching me how to find the beat and move fluidly with the music, without ever saying a word of instruction.

At first, I'm awkward, my face burning bright pink with embarrassment. Everyone around me seems to have taken dance lessons their entire lives or something. They all move freely and smoothly, never missing a single beat, whereas I feel like someone's weird grandpa at a family barbeque.

But gradually, between the little bit of wine I drank and Luca's patient faith in me, I begin to loosen up. And as soon as I turn off my brain and just go with the flow, it's like the music takes over my body, and suddenly I can dance. Maybe not like a professional, but at least nobody is laughing at my awkward moves.

Before long, I'm grinning and laughing, not giving a single damn about who may be watching or judging me.

After all, when I take into stock what's really going on here, how can I be self-conscious?

I'm dancing in a picturesque Italian village with the man of my dreams!

When the song ends, we walk over to a vendor to buy a *cannolo* to share, and on the way to find ourselves a table to sit at, a few men suddenly swarm over to us, laughing and shouting. For a split second, I'm afraid, until I see them all smiling and calling Luca by name. Luca's face lights up when he sees them, opening his arms to embrace each one of them. They begin to speak very quickly in Italian, but I can sort of follow along if I pay attention.

"Luca! Is that really you, my brother?"

"Holy shit, man! You used to be shorter than me, what happened?"

"What are you doing back in Apulia?"

"How long has it been? Ten years?"

Luca answers each of them happily, laughing and clapping them on the shoulder as he reacquaints himself with old friends. If there's one thing I'm figuring out very quickly, it's that Luca was very well-known in these little villages.

When I think about how much of a ballsy troublemaker he was when he was a kid, it makes sense. He's always been so charismatic and fun to be around, of course everyone back home would adore him.

He spends a few minutes chatting with them, introducing me as his fiancée, giving them a very sanitized version of the events which led us here.

Luckily, all his old friends appear to have been drinking, so they don't ask any questions. They just seem happy enough to see Luca again. They don't need all the gritty details.

After a while, they head off, presumably to keep drinking and meet up with some women.

Luca and I eat our dessert, listening to the music while he explains to me how he knows each one of the men who just came up to us. It turns out that most of them were schoolboys together, and they took part in many of Luca's pranks on teachers and other students. He assures me that they never did anything too destructive, but they were definitely not teacher's pets, either.

It's so strange to me, hearing how silly he used to be as a kid. By the time I met him, he was already so mature by comparison to all the guys I had classes with. He seemed like an adult, like he was world-weary and knowledgeable about everything there was to know.

But I guess the life he led, leaving home to work hard for his Uncle Carlo in America, must have changed him. Roughed up those soft edges he used to have. Now that we're so comfortable together, I can see little pieces of that old silliness and light-heartedness shining through sometimes. But it does break my heart to think of how quickly he had to grow up as a teenager. None of it was his fault, but he was the one who paid the price.

The band strikes up another song, this one slower and more romantic. Luca takes my hand and leads me out onto the dance floor again, pulling me close.

We spin slowly together, cheek to cheek, his hand on the small of my back. With the tempo change, most of the single dancers have gone to sit down, leaving just the two of us and a few other couples.

The singer croons about old lovers rediscovering one another, about old vows being renewed, about being together forever and ever in love. It's enough to make my hormonal heart beat a little faster, and I find myself fighting off the tears in my eyes. At the end of the song, Luca kisses me softly on the lips, his hand cradling the back of my head like I'm something delicate, something precious.

He rests his forehead against mine and whispers, "I love you, Serena."

"I love you, too," I answer, smiling.

As we walk off the dance floor, I see several people seated at the tables looking at their partners with lovesick eyes. They scoot closer to each other, hold hands. There's definitely been a shift in mood. Where before the square was filled with high-spirited laughter, now there's a seriousness, a sense of heavy romance in the air. And the two of us are affected the same way.

Luca leads me down the winding streets, away from the bright lights strung up from lamppost to lamppost, away from the music and the smells and the crowds of people. The further we walk, the more alone we are.

We arrive at a lovely, perfectly-manicured little park on the edge of the village. It overlooks the cliff-side below, the hilly fields dotted with grazing animals and flowering bushes. The moon now hangs high in the velvety dark sky, only barely illuminating the face of the man I love, his flawless features nearly glowing before me.

He leans in to kiss me, softly at first, then more passionately. He pulls me in tight, our bodies pressed together so I can feel every rippling muscle. His hands slide down over my hips and around to cup my ass.

His tongue pushes gently into my mouth and I moan, feeling my body warm with excitement at his every touch. His hand roves up my body to grope my breasts, his thumb circling over my nipples, poking through the thin fabric of my dress. I shudder, feeling somehow both weak and powerful in his arms. I don't know how he does what he does to me, but god, I hope he never, ever stops.

He breaks the kiss for a moment, his eyes sparkling as he looks down at me.

There's a question there. My heart starts racing.

I murmur, "Go ahead."

He grins mischievously and scoops me up, carrying me over to the thigh-high stone wall that circle the park and keeps people from falling over the edge and down the cliffside. He sets me down there, wrenching my thighs open with his leg as he kneels down in front of me. I can scarcely breathe, my whole body is on fire, anticipating whatever he's going to do to me.

Some part of me is acutely aware that this is dangerous. I'm literally sitting on the precipice of a painful, terrible fall. And at any moment, someone else could come strolling by and catch us out here, two lovers in the park. But I don't care. The only thing I care about is Luca.

He slides the hem of my dress up my thighs and

hooks a finger under the band of my panties, tugging them down, exposing my sex to the night air. I shudder at the coolness of the breeze, my hands gripping the stone on either side of me. Luca looks up at me with a hungry stare, green eyes shining in the moonlight.

And then he leans in, his tongue flicking over my clit, enveloping my dripping pussy in his warm mouth. I toss my head back and groan, goosebumps prickling up on my arms and legs as he devours me. His tongue pulses in and out of my aching hole, sliding up and down the length of my sex, drinking me in. He plays with my clit, suckling at the tiny bundle of intense nerves until I'm bucking my hips, my hand on the back of his head, holding him there.

"Fuck," I murmur breathlessly, "don't stop, don't stop!"

He nibbles gently at my clit, then sucks it into his mouth, his tongue swirling around it expertly. I whimper, feeling my whole body start to tense up. He always knows just what to do, like he knows my body better than I do. Like I was built for him alone.

Luca spreads my thighs wider and slides one finger inside me, curling it ever so slightly to stroke my g-spot deep inside while his tongue works my clit. The sensation is almost overwhelming, almost enough to make me recoil. But if I withdraw, if I pull back from him, I could fall—down, down the cliff behind me. There's no place else to go. I have to just suck it up and deal with the powerful, intense waves of pleasure radiating through my body.

"Oh my god, oh my god, Luca!" I gasp, closing my eyes as my orgasm mounts. He groans into my pussy, and I can tell he's enjoying this. He loves it: sending me into near-hysterics with that amazing mouth of his. His finger slides in and out of me faster and faster, his tongue circling my clit until I'm almost in tears.

Finally, I erupt into shivers of exquisite bliss, climaxing and gushing sweet honey all over his finger. Luca eagerly licks up every last drop, not even letting up for a moment while my thighs tremble and I whimper incoherently.

He looks up at me, those green eyes fierce, almost frightening in their intensity. He stands up quickly, turns me so that I'm almost lying down on the stone ledge, one foot safely planted on the ground, the other leg dangling off the edge. He unbuckles his jeans, tugs them down along with his boxers.

His cock springs free, long and hard, and I can't help but gasp as he reaches down to rub my clit with his fingers, keeping me slick and wet. He's really going to fuck me right here on the edge of a cliff, in a public park, with a village gathering just streets away from us!

I moan, wriggling toward him, my body aching for him. My heart is pounding, all my senses heightened by the pure danger and thrill of what we're about to do. "Please," I whisper, "do it. Fuck me right here in the open. I need it, Luca. I need you."

He positions the head of his cock at my dripping pussy, sliding it around, teasing me, making me tremble and shake with desire. Leaning over me, he pushes my dress further up to expose my breasts. I've gone without a bra tonight, and at the rush of cool air, my nipples perk up. Still teasing my pussy with the tip of his shaft, he leans down to suck my nipple into his mouth. I groan as his tongue flicks over the stiffened peak, sending spirals of pleasure down between my legs. I roll my hips up against him, begging him to fuck me.

Luca straightens back up, looks me dead in the eye, and slides his cock deep inside me in one smooth thrust. I cry out, and he quickly covers my mouth with his hand as he starts to pump in and down out of my pussy, not even taking the time to go slowly at first. He fucks me fast and hard, slamming into my g-spot again and again as the two of us balance on the edge of the cliff. It almost hurts, but I can't get enough of it. I love the way he's using my body, filling my tight little hole with his engorged shaft like I'm some irresistible fuck-toy.

"Fill me up, Luca. Fuck me. Make me yours," I whisper, feeling the rough stone grinding almost painfully underneath me, chafing my bare skin. But the slight pain almost adds to the pleasure of the moment, and I grit my teeth.

"So good for me, baby," he groans. "Such a tight little pussy. You feel so fucking good."

"Oh god, I love it when you pound into me like this," I murmur, my eyes rolling back in my head. He picks up the pace, fucking me harder and faster, his hips snapping back and forth as he uses my pussy. I'm aching, nearly twitching with bliss, and I cry out again as another climax washes over me. I can feel my pussy pulsing around his cock, squeezing him, bringing him closer and closer to the same edge.

He slams into me with such force I can feel my body scooting closer and closer to the end of the stone ledge, but I don't even care. Fuck, if this is the way I have to go, then it's worth it. I've never felt this exhilarated before, filled with Luca's cock, my pussy aching for him to come inside me and stuff me with his sweet seed. Finally, he rears back and shoves into me with such force he has to grab me and pull me back before I can topple over the edge, and he groans, spilling his thick spunk deep inside my trembling sex.

He holds me close for a moment, letting every last drop of his seed fill me up. He leans down to kiss me fiercely, his tongue shoving into my mouth as his hands grope my breasts, my hips, my ass. After a few moments of this, we hear the distant echo of footsteps approaching. Suddenly remembering where we are and how sticky a predicament we're in, we quickly make ourselves decent and start rushing away from the park, hand-in-hand as we race back to the car.

Laughing with exhilaration, we get in the car and drive home, the car speeding along down the hilly roads. I can still feel his come leaking out of me, staining the brand-new dress I just bought, and it makes me feel satisfied. Complete.

But I'm not quite done with him yet.

We've got a little bit of a drive home to go, and there are almost no streetlights, and no other vehicles in sight. I reach over across the console, rubbing my hand over Luca's softening cock.

He glances at me, confused for half a second, and then realizing what I'm up to. With a devilish grin, I lean over, under his arms, to unzip his jeans and get to his shaft. At my warm breath on his bare skin, his cock starts to stiffen again. I take my time, teasing him with my tongue, sliding my hand up and down his shaft softly until he's completely erect again.

He moans, his hand coming down to rest on the top of my head, gently pushing me down, urging me to suck his cock.

And I gladly oblige.

I pull the head of his stiffened cock into my mouth, letting my tongue flick over the tip before I take him in completely. I almost cough when the head of his cock brushes against the back of my throat, but instead I just start bobbing up and down, fondling the base of his shaft with my hand while I work his hard length.

"Fuck, you're such a dirty, sexy woman," Luca says, just barely thrusting up into my mouth. I tease the head of his cock, licking my lips. I can still taste myself on him.

"I just can't get enough," I whisper, reaching down between my legs to stroke my clit, still dripping with his come. We ride down the highway this way for a while, my mouth sucking his cock, my fingers rubbing my pussy. Every time we go over a bump in the road, his cock slams into the back of my throat—and I love it as much as he does.

I bounce up and down, sucking him off, swirling my tongue around the head, pumping his shaft with my hand. It's not long before I'm climaxing again, moaning as I take Luca's cock deep into my mouth.

"*Brava ragazza*," he murmurs, pushing my head down on his cock. "So good, *dolcezza*."

Just before we pull up to the darkened Lomaglio residence, I suck him harder, bobbing up and down faster and faster until I can feel him tensing up. The car rolls to a stop just as he explodes in my mouth, and I swallow down his come hungrily, licking the tip of his cock. I sit back up, proud of myself, and Luca kisses me, not even caring about the taste of his own come on my lips.

We tumble into bed together, still kissing, ripping off each other's clothes. We explore each other's bodies like it's the very first time, touching and stroking. Before long, he's down between my legs again, licking my pussy and fingering me. Finally, exhausted and spent, we start to drift off in each other's arms, totally happy and blissful.

Just as I'm closing my eyes, a smile still on my lips, my phone buzzes on the bedside table. At first, I decide to just let it go. Let it wait until morning. But something, some instinct without a name, urges me to check it. I reach over in the dark and grab my phone, blinking in the bright light as I read the text message on the screen.

My stomach turns and I start to feel dizzy.

Another message from my mother, finally a reply! But the words make my blood go cold.

Hope you're well. I went out to dinner tonight. Walnuts in the salad.

To most people, this would mean nothing at all. But to me, it's a time machine back to when I was a little kid, to the first time my mother first sent back a plate of food to the kitchen at a fancy restaurant, complaining that there were walnuts in the salad. I was seven years old, and I asked her what the problem was. She explained that she is allergic to walnuts, and so she can't eat them. For some reason, in my child's mind, I took this as some kind of code word for when I didn't like something or didn't want to go through with something.

From then on, whenever I was scared, whenever

I was in trouble, I would use "walnuts" as a code word, a clue to my mother that something was wrong. One time, when I was at a sleepover and I got scared and wanted to go home, I used my friend's parents' phone to call home and whisper, "Walnuts," to my mother. She immediately understood what I meant. She came and picked me up, took me home, giving some believable excuse to my friend's parents about why. My mother and I were never as close as I was with my father, but this was our *thing*.

The day that my first crush was mean to me in eighth grade during gym class, I sent my mom the text message: *Walnuts.* She checked me out for the day, took me shopping, taught me about how boys can be awful sometimes, but I shouldn't let them control how I feel about myself.

Even when I was in high school, trying to get through classes without crying because I was still reeling from the death of my father, I would send my mom the "walnuts" code word to tell her how the day was going, how much I was struggling. When I got older, I used the word less and less often, needing my mother to take care of me less and less.

X was the code word we'd agreed on.

Walnuts was the code word we'd always used.

I know something is wrong. She's in trouble, and she wouldn't use that word without knowing exactly what it would signify to me. I jump out of bed and

start getting dressed, not even sure what I'm planning to do. Luca wakes up and looks over at me,
confused.

"What's going on, *dolcezza*? Are you okay?"

With tears in my eyes, I look back at him and
answer, "We have to leave. My mother is in trouble,
and I have to help her. *Now.*"

I should have been ready. I should have known better. I should have acted sooner. I shouldn't have ignored my instincts.

I will not make such mistakes again.

The SUV races down the highway as fast as I can make the beat-up hunk of metal move. We have no time to waste, and there are few enough police out in the area that I'm not going to worry about going 40-50 miles over the speed limit. A trail of dust runs behind us like a cloud in our wake. I grip the steering wheel so tight that even I notice it.

Serena is in the seat next to me, watching out the window as we barrel down the road.

"Are you sure your friend will have everything ready for us when we get to the air strip?" she asks for the third time, looking over to me with worried eyes.

"If he doesn't, I'll kill him," I say matter-of-factly. Her eyes go wide, but I crack a smile at her to let her know I'm joking. If I don't ease the tension at least a little, we'll both get too strung out to focus, and focus is the one thing we need right now.

"I hope your parents aren't upset we had to leave so fast," Serena says, running her hands through her hair. "I'm so sorry, Luca, we-"

"Don't be sorry," I say, shaking my head, "this is an emergency. We'll be back to see them, and they know my life is...the kind of life that involves sudden changes in plans. It isn't as unusual as you'd think."

She nods, swallowing.

"The plane I have ready for us will get us back to the States faster than any airliner could," I say, watching the strong wind whip sand across the road ahead of us as we make our way toward the air strip. "Once we're onboard, it will be about seven hours straight to New York. I've already reached out to my contacts to have a company car ready for us when we get back."

"The Costas are still looking out for you?"

"I have friends," I say simply. "Friends look out for each other. Besides, I'm a walking symbol by now. It looks good for the Costas for me to stay in good shape, especially when I show up in New York again alive, back from the dead."

I see goosebumps on Serena's arm, and I take my

hand off the stick shift a moment to lay it on hers, giving it a light squeeze.

"Is the family going to be okay here, though?" she asks, her eyes going wide yet again. "If anything were to happen to them because of us…"

"Not gonna happen," I say with a shake of my head. "Now that they have our scent, the only thing these dogs will be interested in is us. Besides, I've warned the village about these outsiders, and the local crime rings are on high alert. The Cleaners have connections in the region, but that's a different matter than a bunch of Americans rolling around causing trouble. And I've had some of my cousins come in to stay with my parents for a week or so, until things cool down. We don't have anything to worry about here."

She nods, looking thoughtful for a few moments. "I want to come back," she says with a determination that I can't help but admire in her. "One day, I mean, when we've gotten through all this. I want to come back and make sure the women's shelter is okay, that they're taken care of. Those women gave me a safe place for as long as they could—I don't know how, but I want to return that kindness."

"I'll make it so," I say with finality, and we exchange a short smile before we turn the corner to the last road we'll take in Italy.

A few minutes later, we pull up the long, open road to where a small private jet is sitting. The tarmac is a small one, really too small for anything to take off from, but it'll have to do for now. I can just barely make out the pilot sitting in the cockpit looking at us approaching through a set of binoculars, and he hails us as we approach.

"Another friend of yours?" Serena asks.

"You don't have anything to do but make friends in this part of the country," I say with a grin. "Well, that and ride cars wildly around the wilderness."

"Right."

The wind is picking up, but the direction it's blowing will only help the plane take off. I drive us not far from the boarding ramp, but my eyes are scanning the area around us.

Something feels wrong.

"I'll get out first," I say calmly, but Serena can pick up on my bad feelings more easily than anyone else. Still, she doesn't question it—she just nods and picks up her bag over her shoulder. "Get out after me. As soon as you're out, stay low and hurry into that plane, understand?"

"Got it," she says. Her eyes look into mine, strong and resolute. I take her hand in mine, bring it to my lips, and kiss it.

I pull the car to a stop, and immediately, I get out of the car, my bag over my shoulder.

I take off my aviators to scan the horizon, eyes moving quickly. There are a lot of cliffs and vantage points from here. No signs of cars rolling our way full of Cleaners, though.

A moment later, I hear Serena's door open, and within a matter of seconds, I see her little form dart from the car up the stairs of the ramp, keeping low, just like I instructed her. My muscles relax a moment later once she's inside the plane.

Then I see it.

Out of the corner of my eye, for barely a fraction of a second, I see the sun glint off something in the cliffs to the south. I'd know a glint like that anywhere.

There's a gunman up there, watching us.

My jaw sets. I should duck and run, make a beeline for the plane, but instead, I step around to the front of the car.

My eyes are set dead-on where I saw the glint. And even from nearly a mile away, I know that I'm staring right back at the barrel of a sniper rifle.

There's no way the Cleaners had enough notice to set up a proper sniper nest this quickly. And I doubt they have many trained sharpshooters in their pocket. That leaves two options in my mind: either someone got lucky and is using that scope to watch us and let his bosses know we're leaving the country, or some young buck is going to try to take the shot.

So I step forward into the open, glaring right back at him.

If you want it so bad, go ahead, try and make the shot.

The wind is bad right now. It doesn't take a marksman to know that a shot at that range with this wind would be a tough one, to say the least. If the man behind that scope has enough skill, though, we're already dead, regardless of whether I run or stand still.

I stand there for a solid ten seconds, my face still as stone, daring him to make the shot. The sun catches the scope again. A quick glint.

Nothing.

My face twists into a frown, and I put my aviators back on. "Coward," I mutter, and I turn my back on the sniper, strutting to the plane and boarding without worry.

"Everything okay?" says my friend in Italian from the cockpit as I enter the plane. Serena is already sitting in one of the comfy seats, looking relieved to see me again.

"All good," I reply, smiling to him warmly. "Hope you can fly in this wind."

"Told you, I was air force," he says with a cocky grin. "And you won't be the first Mafioso I've smuggled out of the country on short notice. Just make sure the cash is in my account, or I'll kick you out over the Atlantic."

We laugh, and I take my seat across from Serena. "Get comfortable," I say, casting one more glance out the window to my homeland. "Before you know it, we'll be back in the Bronx. And we just lost the element of surprise."

~

It turns out that getting comfortable is easier said than done on this flight. Seven hours feels like seven days, and passing the time has proven hard. We don't have much to talk about that doesn't go back to the danger Serena's mother is in, and because of that, it feels a little irreverent to try to focus on the brief good times we've had with my family.

So, three-quarters of the way into the flight, I'm doing push-ups on one hand on the floor of the cabin. Serena watches me, if only to distract herself from the stress.

It isn't working so well.

As for me, I have to stay in peak physical condition, no matter what. This isn't a serious workout for me, just something to keep me warmed up, because for all I know, we could be landing in the middle of a firefight.

Until this is finished, I need to be beyond my A-game, and lying on my ass in a hospital bed didn't help my strength.

"But what if it's too late?" Serena says anxiously, and it's not the first time she's expressed that fear. I can't blame her. The situation isn't good. "What if something's happened to her already? Oh my god, I've just been goofing off like I'm on some vacation all this time and I'm the worst daughter ever. Or what if *nothing* bad has happened to her and someone stole her phone and is luring us into a trap and-"

"Then I will kill them," I say simply, lowering myself to the ground before putting both hands down to push myself up. I stride over to her, crouching beside her seat and taking her hand reassuringly. I'm bare-chested, having taken my shirt off to exercise more easily.

"Serena," I say in a low tone, looking into those anxious eyes, on the verge of tears for hours now. "You can't be everywhere at once. You had to run for your life. You ran for the child's life. You did the right thing—you kept yourself alive. If your mother isn't the kind of person who can recognize how important that is, then she's no mother at all."

Her face just watches me, trembling, and I know the great beast of fear within her is trying to push out any hope of comfort. I rise up and sit in the seat next to her, raising the armrest to pull her close to my chest, letting her head rest there.

"I don't know if I could forgive myself if something happened, though," she whispers.

"I know, *passerotta*," I say, stroking her hair gently with my thick fingers. "But we've gone through a trial of fire, both of us—and you're not used to this.

What you've accomplished, what you've *survived* in Italy is a greater feat of strength than I could ever come close to."

"I don't know about that," she says with a soft smile.

"We're coming back from the dead, you and me," I say, looking down to that face I love so strongly. "You're doing all this for your family, nothing else. It would be enough for your mother for you to keep yourself and your future child safe, but going back to look after family? If that doesn't make you a good daughter, I don't know what does."

After a moment, she looks up at me with a struggling smile on her face, and she gets closer to me. My arms, warm from exercise, wrap around her comfortingly, and we hug with nothing but the droning of the plane all around us for a few moments.

"You are my strength, Serena," I say, squeezing her gently. "I mean that. We have each other, and that makes us strong enough to move mountains for what we love."

Just then, I hear the pilot's voice over the speaker.

"Luca, just to let you know, we just crossed into radius of American phone signals. If you have any calls to make, now's the time."

"Thanks," I call to the cockpit, and I nod to Serena, standing up and getting a phone from my bag.

A few moments later, the phone is ringing, and I'm pacing the cabin with a hand on my hip.

"...hello?" an uncertain voice answers from the other end.

"Hello, Giovanni," I say with a grin. "Nice to hear you again."

"Holy shit, Luca," Giovanni gushes, laughing at the other end of the line. "Don't give me a heart attack like that! Fuck, it's good to hear from you. You really didn't waste any time stirring up the goddamn wasp's nest coming back to life, huh? Rising on the third day too good for you?"

"It's a bad habit," I say, winking at Serena.

"Where are you?" he asks. "Can you even answer that? What's going on?"

"We're heading back to America," I say. "We'll be in the Bronx before the end of the day. I need you to make sure pickup arrangements are settled at the air strip. You know the one. I've already got some guys on it, but I want someone I trust there with them. Talk to Nico."

"You got it," Giovanni says, and I can still hear the disbelief through the phone. "I gotta say, Luca, it's fuckin' weird hearing your voice again. I mean, I'd heard rumors, but..."

"This is on a need-to-know basis," I say. "Trust me, if I'd wanted to go public with this, you'd be one of the first men I contacted. But what's this about rumors? What's the situation in the Bronx?"

"Shit, you don't know anything, do you?" Giovanni says in wonder.

"I've had a bad case of the 'dead,' Giovanni."

"Right, right. Well, things are uh, not good. We're in an all-out mob war, Luca."

I clench my jaw. "The Cleaners don't know when to die, do they?"

"They were backed into a corner for a while there, but anything backed into a corner fights hard. When everyone thought you'd been killed, they fought twice as hard to get back lost territory. Lot of good men are dead. It's been a bloody winter and a bloodier spring. Nobody even knows what the turf borders are anymore, it feels like every week some block is ours, then it's the Cleaners, you get the idea. Don Abruzzi dug his heels in hard, and he's holding the vendetta for his son's death against the whole Costa family. He circulated a bunch of news about your death, too, saying he had your body, photos, all kinds of shit."

I listen to all this with a still expression, taking it all in. When he's finished, I take a breath.

"Alright. Giovanni, I want you to get the boys back together. Only the men I've been on jobs with, you know the ones. Men we can trust. I'll explain more when we land, but the Cleaners probably know by now that I'm going to be back in town soon. I'm going to lead us on a job."

"A job? Shouldn't we touch base with Don Costa?"

"Fuck the Don," I grunt. "Has he given a shit when I've been busting my ass across the world on their account? No. You know who has stuck up for us? *Us*, Giovanni. If we want something done right, we do it ourselves. This is our neighborhood. Not the Cleaners', and not the Don's. I'll deal with the blowback later, if anyone wants to cross that bridge. You with me or not?"

There's a long sigh from the other end of the line before Giovanni says, "Shit, yeah, you know I'm with you, Luca. Alright, let's do this. I'll see you in a few."

I end the call, and I look down to Serena, who looks shocked at me.

"Did I just hear all that right?"

"I didn't survive a car bomb to go back to following orders like a grunt," I say.

"Well, yeah," she says with a smile, but it fades as she goes on, "I mean, what did you mean, 'job'? What are you planning?"

A cocky smile crosses my face. "We're going to find your mother by drawing the bastards out of hiding first. And we're going to do that by finishing this where it started."

The car rolls to a stop just down the block, and it hits me how strange it is to be surrounded by these familiar sights again. Italy feels like a world away, like a dream I wish I could get back to. Those sweet, happy memories are fading away, almost like it never happened at all. It's heartbreaking, but at the same time, I know there's a lot I need to get done here. I can't just live in denial forever while the world keeps burning down everything I've built around me.

Maybe someday things will be soft and easy again, but now is not that time.

Now, it's time for action.

I hop out of the car before Luca can even turn off the engine, and I start marching my pregnant self down the street, my stomach churning and my heart racing. As I approach the building where Bathing

Beauty is located, I nearly double over to throw up at the sight of it.

My beautiful store, the shop I have worked so hard for, is in shambles.

There are streamers of yellow caution tape all over the entrance, the windows busted up and cracked, tiny splinters of glass littering the sidewalk. I cover my mouth with my hands in shock, stepping gingerly through the broken glass to the front door. With a shaking hand, I take the key out of my pocket and fit it in the door. I have to jostle it to try and get it open, since the door is hanging slightly crooked on its hinges, like it's been knocked off-angle. Like somebody kicked the door in to break inside the shop. To my surprise and panic, the key doesn't quite fit like it used to. I thought it was opening up, but apparently the door is just so messed up that it can't open anymore like it used to. Luca comes up behind me and takes my hand.

"Come on, *mia passerotta*. I'll get us in somehow," he tells me gently. He leads me around the back of the building, to the rear employees' entrance. As expected, my key doesn't fit here either, but luckily Luca has enough brute strength to break through the door, shattering the lock in the process. I rush inside and start turning on the lights—half of which don't turn on, and the other half only flicker pathetically, like they've been smashed to bits.

As I walk through the kitchen and storage rooms, I can feel a lump rising in my throat.

The shelves are all knocked over, chemicals and equipment scattered all over the floor. Luca grabs me by the arm and says, "Be careful, Serena. I don't think you should be here, breathing in these chemicals. It's not safe for you or the baby."

"Just... just let me look around a little bit. I-I need to take stock of things," I say, my voice already shaky. Leaning on Luca for support, I walk through to the main shop front, my breath catching in my lungs as I take in the horrific scene. The state of things is even worse in here. All the cabinets and shelves have been ripped out of the walls. All the products are smashed and poured on the floor. The files are spread out everywhere, some of them ripped to pieces. All my hard work is lying here in bits on the ground, unceremoniously dumped out and trampled on.

I immediately start to cry, unable to hold back the waterworks. The waves of devastated emotion crash over me and I crumple to the floor, burying my face in my hands. I sob openly, feeling my heart shatter into a million pieces. First, I learned that my mother is missing and most certainly in danger, and now my beloved shop, the business I've worked so hard to keep going, is destroyed. My family's last asset, our last hope, dashed to pieces by the enemy.

Luca rushes over to comfort me, tugging me into his arms and kissing my forehead.

"I'm so sorry, Serena," he murmurs. "Those bastards are going to pay for this. I promise."

"Everything I had here is ruined. My old life—I'm so stupid. I abandoned it all. I was having such a wonderful time in Italy with you, and I was so selfish to think I could just leave it all behind and it would be okay. I'm an idiot. I shouldn't have just let it all go so easily. I should have been here to make things right," I sob angrily, shaking my head. "I'm so mad at myself. I can't believe I let this happen."

"Serena, stop. This isn't your fault. You didn't choose to leave, *dolcezza*. Remember? You had to go. It was the only way to save you and the baby. You did what you had to do to survive."

"Yeah? And now what? My mother is in trouble, the shop is ruined, and I can't do anything to fix it. I've made such a mess of everything, Luca, and I don't know what to do!"

He helps me stand up and leads me over to sit down on a stool miraculously left standing behind the beaten-up cashier counter. He kisses me on the cheek. "Just sit here for a minute. Breathe slowly. It's going to be okay. I'm going to *make* this okay. Just trust me."

I sit there, breathing deeply, doing what I'm told, because… well, what the hell else can I do anyway? The tears slowly begin to subside and I calm down a little bit, coming out of the darkness to notice that Luca is going around the room with a garbage bag, cleaning up as he goes.

"What are you doing?" I ask, frowning.

"Cleaning up. Just like old times," he says, giving me a reassuring smile.

Despite how awful everything is, I can't help but smile back weakly. "What's the point, Luca? This place is a mess. It's shut down. There's no hope for Bathing Beauty. This shop has been beaten down and vandalized and destroyed so many times by now, what's the use?"

"Well, I'm not giving up. Not yet. We've rebuilt this place before, and we can sure as hell do it again, Serena," he says. He walks over to me and takes my hands, kneeling in front of me. "Listen to me, okay? This is important. You can't stay here. It's not safe. All these crazy chemicals in the air have got to be dangerous for you and the baby. I have a plan, but you have to trust me and do what I say. Alright?"

I look at him suspiciously.

"What exactly am I agreeing to?"

He sighs.

"Serena. I have a lot to get done here."

"What is your plan? You have to tell me, Luca."

He hesitates for a moment and I add, "I'm the mother of your child. I'm your fiancée. You and me? We're a team. That means you have to keep me in the loop."

Luca smiles again, shaking his head.

"God, you're stubborn. But you're right. Okay." He takes a deep breath and continues, "Here's what's going to happen. I'm going to clean this place up, get the lights back on, make it look like it's up and running again."

"But why? Won't that just make the Cleaners suspicious?" I ask.

He nods.

"Exactly. But it won't just make them suspicious, it will make them angry. It will draw them out, get them to come here and try and put us back in our place."

"Luca…" I breathe, my eyes going wide. "Are you really setting a trap? That isn't a good idea. It isn't safe."

He kisses my hand.

"Yes. But the time for playing it safe has passed. And besides, I won't be alone here. The Cleaners think we're alone, you and me. They think we're free agents. I made sure to spread word around town, get the rumor mill started on telling everybody that I quit. Broke away from the Costa family for good. The Cleaners will think I'm severely outmanned here. But what they won't know is that there will be Costa members hiding in wait all around here. The Cleaners won't send the big guns in to get me—they won't see any reason to. So when they show up, *they'll* be the ones outnumbered, outgunned."

"That's crazy, Luca. You can't do this," I tell him firmly, shaking my head. "It's too risky. You know that. I-I can't let you do this."

"Serena, it's the only way. If you've got a better plan, let's hear it."

I sit silently, my mouth closing as I realize he's right. I don't have any other ideas.

He cups my face in his hands.

"*Dolcezza,* I can do this. I've faced worse enemies than these before. Do you trust me?"

I nod.

"You know trust isn't the problem. I trust you with my life."

"You're just going to have to let me do this, even if it scares you. I promise it will work. It will all be just fine in the end," he assures me. "But you can't stay here. I won't let you become a casualty of this war. It's my fight, Serena, not yours."

"What do you mean? I'm not leaving you here. Bathing Beauty is my responsibility. And you— you're my fiancé. I can't just abandon you when you need me!" I exclaim.

Luca pulls me into a tight hug. "I can only do this if I know you're somewhere else—somewhere safe. I will not let them anywhere near you. I'm the prize in this honeypot, not you."

"Where will I go?" I ask, shaking my head as my eyes fill with tears again.

"Rafaela's. She's coming to get you any minute now."

Just as the words leave his mouth, there's the honk of a car horn outside. I look back over my shoulder and see Rafaela in Nico's car, looking very solemn and pale.

"Luca, don't do this," I beg, clinging to him desperately.

"It will all be okay," he says, nearly dragging me out the door. I continue to cry and protest as he pulls me around to the front of the building, taking out his phone to make a quick call. "Giovanni. *Si.* Tonight. Go ahead and send them. It'll all be in place by then."

He gently pushes me into the passenger seat, then looks up at Rafaela and says, "Take care of her. Make sure she eats. And drinks water. And make sure she relaxes—"

"Got it," Rafaela says curtly, nodding. "You do what you have to do."

"Luca!" I cry out tearfully. "Don't you dare."

"*Mia passerotta*, I will see you when the smoke clears. I love you," he says, leaning through the window to kiss me even as the tears streak down my cheeks.

Rafaela throws the car into gear and we take off down the street. I glance back, seeing Luca's shape getting smaller and smaller until he disappears. I turn to Rafaela, who is staring stony-faced at the road.

"Take me back!" I shout at her. She shakes her head. I can tell this is incredibly hard for her. She doesn't like having to drag me away against my will. "Rafaela, turn this car around."

"No!" she barks back. "No. I can't do that, Serena. You're my best friend and I love you and I'd do anything for you, but this? This is out of our hands."

"Please, Raf. I can't just leave him back there. Not —not again," I whisper, thinking back to riding in this car as it sped away from the explosion, leaving the love of my life behind.

There are tears in her big brown eyes. "*Hermana,* no. This is my part in the fight, okay? There isn't much I can do. Nico and all the others—they can fight. But I'm no fighter, Serena. This—taking care of you—this is the only way I can contribute. I have to do what I'm told."

"You don't understand," I whimper.

She stops the car suddenly, turning to me with flashing, angry eyes.

"*I* don't understand? *Amiga,* I know exactly what you feel! Do you think I don't break down and cry every time Nico goes out to do god-knows-what for the mafia? Do you think I haven't been worried sick with panic the whole time you've been off in Italy? I had no idea whether you were alive or dead all that time! Do you really think I don't know what you're going through? I was there, too! I saw that explosion! And the whole time I just kept thinking, 'That could have been Nico. That could have been Serena. Hell, that could have been me.' Don't you understand that I've been terrified, too? Serena, you know me better than that. You're like a sister to me, and this is the one way I can do my part. Just let me do my part," she says, her lip trembling as she bursts into tears, too.

"Oh god, I'm so sorry, Raf," I mutter, reaching over to hug her.

"I've been so scared, Serena. I thought my best friend was gone forever," she cries.

"If I had been able to reach out to you, I would have. You know that, right?" I assure her.

"I know, I know."

"I can't imagine how scary it was for you, being stuck here, not knowing what was going on," I tell her, and I mean it. Guilt floods into my heart. I hadn't even thought about it. Poor Rafaela, worried half to death all this time.

"All along, I've just been quiet, doing what they tell me to do. I used to think I was pretty tough, you know? I thought I was strong. But this stuff? It's way over my head," she sniffles.

"Rafaela, you are strong. You always have been. It's scary, but you're still here. Right? You're surviving! And thank god, too, because I don't know what

I'd do if anything happened to you," I confess. She wipes her eyes.

"I'm sorry for blowing up at you like that, but I've just been so wound up, so tense all the time waiting for the next shoe to drop," she says, trying to calm herself down.

"I know the feeling. It's okay. You have every right to feel that way."

"Dios mío, I just hate standing on the sidelines, knowing I can't do anything to help. You know? It's awful. I want to do more, but there's nothing I can do," she laments, frustrated.

"You know, we don't have to just go sit and wait like the guys tell us to," I begin cautiously, not wanting to upset her further. "We don't have to just watch while the men we love go charging half-cocked into battle. We can help."

"How? How the hell can we do anything?" she asks, looking at me sideways.

"We refuse to sit on our hands and wait for everything to be okay. We join the ranks and we *make* it okay. We fight," I suggest.

"What are you saying?" she says, frowning at me.

I take a deep breath.

"We go back."

"Be straight with me, Luca," says Giovanni, peering out the open door with a cigarette hanging out of his mouth while he loads his pistols. "Think they'll take the bait?"

"Have you seen any cops roll by in the past two hours?" I reply, my arms crossed as I watch with him.

"Nah."

"There's your answer. This is a challenge, and they've accepted it."

"Fuck me," he says, flicking his cigarette out onto the street and flashing a half-grin at me, "I forgot how dramatic things could get with you around."

Bathing Beauty looks like it's back in business. We've torn down all the boards from the windows, dusted off everything, gotten the power back on, and even turned some of the lights on. It's late by now, and most of the other shops on the block have shut down. The fact that this place is a glowing beacon of light makes it look conspicuous already.

When I said it was a challenge, I meant it. There aren't many people tied to the mafia who don't know about this place by now. First it was the place Serena, last of the De Laurentis mob royalty, was supposed to live out a quiet life, an old front turned legit. Then it became known as the beginning of the end for Lorenzo Abruzzi after he tried to get Serena to pay protection and I showed up. When I was in jail, the Cleaners didn't forget about this place. Seeing it all but shut down must have been like a monument to their victory after they thought they killed me.

I couldn't have sent a stronger message if I'd thrown a glass of wine in Don Abruzzi's face.

Giovanni and I walk away from the windows and move back to the main floor of the shop, where we've got my own little army with us. Eleven men in total, not counting me. We've got a scout watching the roads for us to give us the heads up.

Most of these men are low-ranking guys. Guys I've done jobs with, some of them who still can't believe their eyes when they look at me walking and breathing, still alive. One of them even saw the car bomb go off.

And they're my people, as far as I'm concerned. A few of them have girlfriends of their own back home who don't know whether they're going to come home tonight. Some of them won't, but it'll get even worse if we don't take a stand now. The bosses don't care about that. They only care about their money.

Me, I'm interested in protecting the neighborhood.

My phone buzzes, and I put it to my ear.

"Three cars on their way. Get ready."

"Good," I grunt, and no sooner have I hung up the phone than I realize the whole room is looking at me, waiting for a word. I'm not one to give speeches.

"Three tin cans full of dead men are rolling our way," I announce, taking out my guns and casting a hard gaze over all of them. "They're on their way to try to fill this place with bullet holes and make this neighborhood their own, and they're not gonna stop until all of you are dead. But I just dragged my ass across five thousand miles of ocean with them on my heels, and believe me when I tell you they're not half the hot shit they think they are."

A few of the men give resolute nods.

"I know you all. Lucca, I still got the smell of your uncle's barbecue in my jacket. Frankie, I've still got the scar from when we worked on our first car in the junkyard. Mario, you still owe me a beer, and hell is a dry county, so we're not going down without it."

They laugh, and I glance over my shoulder as the

sound of rolling tires on asphalt reaches my ear. I look back to all of them with a serious expression.

"And I sure as hell didn't come back from the goddamn dead to get shot up by these punks again. Showtime, men, let's give 'em hell!"

Dressed in a dusty leather jacket, black shirt that won't show blood as easily, dirty blue jeans, and black boots, I move behind an island counter in the middle of the shop, feeling like I'm holding the center in a battlefield. Some of the men are behind the checkout counter. Others are behind walls, crouching or standing, all toting guns and all ready for action.

The door is open. It looks like an invitation, but I had something else in mind.

With headlights off, the three black sedans roll into view, windows down, men packed into them. They roll up toward the building, and before one of them can even think to lean out and start taking shots, I take action.

I pop up from hiding and fire a round straight into a tire of the front car.

Immediately, it skids, taking the passengers by surprise, and the men take that as cue to start firing. We won't be sitting ducks for this one.

As bullet holes start appearing in the cars and ricocheting off, Cleaners start pouring out of the opposite doors and taking positions behind their cars. They know they can't stay there for long, though. It's only a matter of time before someone hits a gas tank, and while the police might be paid off to keep clear, an explosion like that won't be one they can ignore.

My men are good shots. As the Cleaners dart for cover, firing rounds into the shop and shattering the glass of the windows, Giovanni downs one of them with a shot to the throat while another of my men lands a clean shot through the heart of another.

The bullet holes appearing in the shop tell me they're packing some heavy heat. Still, the men are managing to hold them down, and they're not about to gain ground on us anytime soon. The only question will be whether or not they're able to make a push inward once—

"Luca!" Giovanni yells, interrupting my thoughts. I look over at him as I get back down to cover, and he points to the third car.

It's still moving. And it's headed around to the back of the shop.

"Are they trying to fucking flank us?" he shouts, and I waste no time in taking aim at the moving car. Its tires are shot to hell, but it's still heading around. Whoever's in there is determined to get the drop on us if it's the last thing that car does.

Two of my rounds fire into the backseat before a bullet grazes my forearm and I'm forced to withdraw, gritting my teeth.

"You got one, maybe two," Giovanni shouts, "let's get some men back there!"

"No!" I grunt in reply. "Give any ground here, and they'll overwhelm us. I'll handle this one myself. Cover me!"

I don't give Giovanni time to reply, but the men overheard me. They start concentrating fire to give me cover as I roll out from behind the counter. When I get back to my feet, both guns are out, and I unload into the other cars, watching men taking cover behind dumpsters as the cars take heavy hits.

It looks like I'm firing wildly, but every shot is measured. I've gotten skilled at this over the years, and my exercise hasn't failed me. I watch no less than three men go down before I force myself to focus on my objective again.

I head to the back room.

If the third car was heading around back, they'll be coming in from the rear entrance. I have a man back there just in case, but he won't be enough to handle a car full of men.

When I appear in the back room, my guard looks at me with anticipation. "I heard shit going down out front, where do you want me?"

"Up there with them," I say, clapping him on the back. "I've got this."

"You sure, Luca?"

"I'm always sure."

He nods and follows my orders, leaving me alone

in the room. I know I have all of about ten seconds to prepare.

That's enough time to reload my guns.

I can hear feet running outside, and my eyes dart around the room. I have no time for intricate traps. What I *do* have is a rack full of old cleaning and soap making supplies near the door. It's not elegant, but it'll do. I can push it onto whoever piles inside and at least get the element of surprise on my side. I pull it away from the wall and position it to face the door from the side.

But before I can get it just the way I want it, the door gets yanked open, and I see the arms of a man holding a gun appear in the doorway from my angle.

Fuck it.

I simply raise my gun and blow his hands off at the wrist.

Through the howl of pain, I shove a large jug of lye off the shelf and into the doorway just as bullets start peppering it.

The caustic liquid pours out, and I hear a few yelps of pain as the men scramble back, giving me just enough of an in to make my move.

I appear in the doorway the next moment, and three shots later, the two gunmen and the one on the ground slump against the wall of the alley behind the store, blood running from shots to the head.

Three dead here, one killed in the car...

I'm missing one.

And that instinct tells me to dive half a second before the fifth man springs out of hiding behind a dumpster to fire at me as he rolls, just as I did less than a minute ago.

He's tall, heavily built, and he knows how to move. This is no ordinary mafia soldier.

When I get back to my feet, he's doing the same, but we're at too close range to shoot at each other. He tries to whip me across the head with the butt of his weapon, but I drop my guns and catch him by the wrist and deliver a hard hit to his stomach.

He's hard as a rock, and he brings his head crashing down to mine. It stuns me, to my surprise, but I squeeze his wrist until he drops the gun with a grunt of pain.

He tries to bring his head down to hit mine again, but this time, I release him and back up, kicking his gun across the alley. We freeze for a moment, staring at one another with bloodlust in our eyes, arms out and ready.

Then his face twists into a sneer.

"Never thought I'd get to look you in the eyes, Luca Lomaglio," he says.

"I look everyone I kill in the eyes," I say as I wipe a trickle of blood away from my forehead. "Have we met?"

"Nah," he says with a casual laugh, "but you made me a rich man. Remember that raid on the junkyard fight all those years ago that was supposed to get your ass killed?" He winks at me. "I was the Costa insider that helped set you up. The Abruzzi family pays a hell of a lot better, you know. Not that it matters now."

My jaw clenches.

"So, when I kill you, it'll be for each of the men who died that night." I lunge at him, and he rolls out of the way and catches me under my ribs. I grunt, but I strike back with my elbow and catch him on the chin.

He stumbles back, then lunges at me with both hands, and we grapple. He thrusts me against the wall behind us, and he tries to land a punch on my face, but I bring my whole head forward to connect my forehead to his nose. He howls in pain and staggers back, and I take my chance.

I rush forward and catch him around the waist, bringing him to the ground with a hard thump. But this guy's more nimble than he looks. I try to get up on him to start pounding his face into the ground, but he twists and throws a punch right at my nose that I have to roll off him to dodge. Both of us on the ground, he swings his leg around to bring it down like an axe on me, but I catch it, holding up an immense amount of force that went into the blow, gritting my teeth.

I twist his leg until he howls, but he lifts his other leg and lands a blow in my chest that pushes me back and off him.

That's when I feel something cool against my hand. It's of the guns that I dropped when we started this fistfight.

Moving as fast as I can force my body to, I snatch the pistol up and get to my feet, pointing the gun directly at my opponent…

…and I find myself looking straight back at the barrel of my other gun, held in his hands, trained on me.

Both of us freeze. He's on the ground, aiming up at me, and I'm not budging an inch from him. We're locked in a standoff.

There's no sound in the alleyway besides our heavy panting and the ringing in our ears.

And at the same time, both of us realize why that's odd.

"The fighting's over out front," he growls.

"Sure is," I grunt back, my finger on the trigger. "That means this standoff will be pointless in a few seconds."

"Yeah," he says, eyes narrowing and a smirk growing on his face. "That leaves us one question: which side won?"

On cue, a voice barks from the other end of the alley behind me.

"Drop the gun, asshole!"

My muscles tense for a moment.

Then a stupid grin crosses my face while his

vanishes. Slowly, he sets his gun on the ground and raises his hands as footsteps behind me approach.

And Serena appears at my side, a gun held out in front of her in shaky hands.

"I thought I told you to stay away," I say, but it's in an almost playful tone. I should have known better than to think she'd stay put. And fuck, I'm glad she didn't.

Still, she gives me a deserved kick in the shin. "Get your finger off the trigger too, hun."

"What? Why?"

Serena takes aim at the man, fire in her eyes. "Because I don't want you to kill him before he tells us where the fuck my mom is."

I can't believe I did that.

I cannot. Believe. I did that.

Looking down at the shiny weapon in my lap, I gulp down my panic. I, Serena De Laurentis, a girl who used to get woozy at the sight of blood, who used to not even be able to handle watching action movies if they got too intense—I just held a man at gunpoint.

Who the hell am I anymore?

I look up and out the window of the back seat of the stolen car, watching the city pass by, the buildings getting smaller and farther apart until we're way down the highway, leaving the skyscrapers behind. Leaving the shop, the one I've sweated and cried over, behind. Leaving the scene of a bloodbath. A battlefield.

The words stumble out of my mouth out loud this time: "I can't believe I did that."

"Serena," says Luca softly. "Serena, look at me."

I slowly drag my eyes away from the window, turning to gaze at Luca's face in the rearview mirror. It's still jarring to see him wearing the clothes of the man I held at gunpoint. After I finished interrogating the guy, Luca made him switch jackets and give up his hat. He's got the collar up and the hat pulled low, almost over his green eyes, to disguise himself.

He looks concerned as he stares at me in the mirror, but still gleaming with something like pride. I can't believe what I'm seeing. He's actually proud of me for what I did back there.

"Hmm?" I manage to mumble through my stupor of shock.

"Are you okay? *Dolcezza*, talk to me."

"I just pointed a gun… this gun," I begin, nodding at the weapon in my lap, "at a person. Like, a living person. I just threatened a man with a gun."

"Yes. You did."

"While I'm pregnant."

"Yes. That's… that's true."

"I-I can't help feeling like that's going to have some kind of, I don't know, effect on the baby. Like, it's going to be born with this inherent bloodlust or something," I confess.

Luca looks at me sideways, clearly trying not to smirk.

"Serena, you did what you had to do. And it worked. Because of you, we now know where they're keeping your mother. We know where we have to go to rescue her. You did that. You made that happen," he says, shaking his head in awe. "Now, do I want you to ever do that shit again? No. Hell, no. After all this is over, I never want that kind of violence anywhere near you or the baby. But Serena, listen to me. You did the right thing. You got the information we need. And you didn't shoot the guy."

"Yeah, but he didn't know I wouldn't," I say, trembling a little. "Shit. *I* didn't even know if I wouldn't. What does that say about me?"

"It says you're one tough lady, and you're loyal and brave as anyone I've ever known. It says that when shit gets hard, you pull yourself together and you make things happen. It means that you'd do anything for family. For love. And that, *mia passerotta*, is what I love most about you."

He looks over at me, just the hint of a smile playing on his lips.

"Now, what I need you to do for me is stay angry. Don't let fear or guilt overcome you right now. There will be time to reflect on your decisions later. Right now, I need for you to get really, really pissed off. These people have fucked with the wrong woman, right?" he says, trying his best to amp me up.

But truthfully, he doesn't need to. Because underneath my shaky hands and my nervousness, I *am* pissed. I'm furious.

Those bastards not only destroyed my store, unhinged my life, tried to kill the man I love, terrified my friends, and put my baby in danger, but now… they've messed with my *mom?* Trading her around like some pawn, like she's a prisoner of war, just a commodity to be tossed back and forth between both sides?

Hell no.

Not *my* mom. We may not have the closest mother-daughter relationship in the world, but we're still family.

Back at the women's shelter, I saw all kinds of girls down on their luck, pushed aside, battered, whittled down, forgotten about. Nobody was going to look out for them but us. Nobody looked out for me there but my fellow women.

I know if Luca had been there, he would have protected me—but he hardly needed to. Those women saved me, built me back up after I thought I lost everything. If there's one thing my time at the shelter taught me, it's that women have to stick together, regardless of our differences.

And that includes my mom.

She's still the one who raised me, who helped me become the woman I am today. She loves me, and I love her, and I'll be damned if I let the Cleaners hurt her.

Especially because they know exactly who she is. They know exactly where she came from.

Her family name used to mean something to these people.

They used to fear the Gaspari name. Her father—my grandfather—was a revered member of the community. Those same guys who are holding her captive now used to whisper among each other about how my mom was uptight. Frigid. Snobby. They thought she needed to be brought down a peg, taught a lesson.

Well, not today. For all her faults, my mother is not the cold bitch they think she is, and even if she was, who could blame her? Living in a man's world, surrounded by all these men, including her only family members, who treated her like a pet or a trading asset. I remember the way my dad used to talk about how all his buddies back in the day said he was crazy for marrying her, that she was too full of herself. Too uppity.

I remember what my dad said to me: "Show me a man who says he won't marry a strong-willed woman, and I'll show you a man who is too weak to deserve her in the first damn place."

She went on living and doing her thing long after my father died, after his debts came to light, after everything fell apart. She could have run away and hid, licked her wounds in the shadows.

But no.

She was too strong, too proud to give up that easily. My mother knew as well as I did what kinds of awful things they all said about her, about us. And she didn't let any of them drag her down. I will defend her until the end, because maybe the reason we don't get along very well is that we're just too alike. Two strong-willed women who fall in love with the only men who are strong enough to handle us.

I smile to myself.

"Don't worry, Mom. I'm on my way," I murmur.

After a while, we pull up to a truck stop wait out in the middle of nowhere. The street lights only flicker dimly, as though nobody really cares enough to fix them out here. As we turn down the gravel way, Luca flashes the headlights in the direction of a big truck waiting there. It flashes back at us. Go time.

"Here we go," Luca says quietly. He tugs the hat a little further down on his head. Two Cleaners in similar dark jackets and hats get out of the other truck and start walking our way. I slink down in the back seat, hiding myself from sight in the darkness. The last thing we need is for the Cleaners to recognize me and catch on to our ruse. I can hear their footsteps splashing through the puddles on the ground. My heart starts racing.

"Are you sure about this?" I ask, barely even loud enough to hear.

"Too late to back out now," Luca answers at the same volume.

"What are you going to do?"

"This will require… a delicate touch."

"What does that mean—"

Just then, the car door flings open and I hear two shots ring out with an earsplitting crack. Against my better judgment, I sit straight up and look around, desperately hoping the shots came from Luca and not from the Cleaners. Relief floods over me as I see Luca pointing his gun at a guy on the ground, cowering next to the man bleeding out beside him. Neither of them look mortally wounded, just shot in the legs to keep them still.

Without another moment of hesitation, I burst out of the car and start bolting toward the Cleaners' truck, hardly thinking about the concern that there might be more of them lying in wait just in case something goes wrong. I don't see anyone else around, so I quickly throw open the front cabin of the truck, take the keys from the ignition, and run to the back. With one hand still gripping the gun, I use my other hand to shakily put the key in the lock, throwing open the back of the truck. I point the gun into the darkness, just in case there might be another man waiting there to shoot me first.

Then I hear it—a scream from the darkness.

A woman's scream.

"Serena?!"

A human shape comes fumbling out of the dark cargo bed—the shape of my mother. She looks bedraggled and angry and a little shocked, but it's definitely her.

"Serena, is that a *gun?*" she gasps.

I can't help but burst out laughing, both relieved and amused by the ridiculousness of my mother's question. "Oh my god. Yes, Mom. This is a gun."

I help her out of the truck and, setting the gun down on the ground, throw my arms around her in the tightest, most genuine hug I've ever given her. "Mom, I'm so glad you're okay!" I cry.

"Oh, I'm okay. I could definitely use a bath, though. These filthy men have never seen a bar of soap in their lives, I bet," she scoffs, already back to her old self.

I kiss her on the cheek.

"Yeah, I think cleanliness is pretty low on their list of priorities, despite their name," I agree, laughing as I take her hand and lead her back around. She gasps again at the sight of the Cleaners on the ground, now being tied up together with rope, courtesy of Luca. He comes over and offers my mother his arm, which she hesitantly takes to lean on.

As we walk back to the car and get inside, she looks him up and down.

"So you're the man who's responsible for all this," she says coyly, gesturing toward my pregnant belly.

"Mom! He's also the man responsible for saving your ass," I retort.

She turns on me, her eyes flashing.

"You think I don't know what kind of man this is? I was married to the mafia! Hell, I was born into it just as you were! Serena, do you remember how often your father was away? How long we would wait for him to come home? How many days he would go out and not call? Maybe you don't remember—you were just a child. But I remember everything. I remember waiting up all night for him to come home, to call and let me know he was alive, at the very least."

She takes a deep breath, smoothing her hair back from her face.

"The point is, my dear, you must be careful. Both of you. I will not watch you struggle the way I have," she says to me emphatically. I step forward and take her arm gently.

"I know. And trust me, I have an entirely different life planned for us. For me and for the baby. Your grandchild isn't going to live in that world. I promise," I assure her.

Seemingly satisfied with my response, she turns back to Luca.

"And you! I can tell you're a capable man. But you have that look of danger about you. I know that look. Listen to me very carefully: this girl, my daughter, is my heart and soul. If you ever put her life in danger again, I will make sure you regret it for the rest of your life," she says, her prim and proper tone in direct opposition to the ferocity of her words. My jaw drops. I have never heard my mother speak that way.

Luca smiles good-naturedly.

"Yes, ma'am. I understand. Your daughter has changed my life. She's made me a far better man than I ever was before. I intend to spend the rest of my days protecting her and making her happy. Serena is my fiancée. And we would be married by now if not for… extenuating circumstances. I can assure you that is my top priority once everything gets sorted out," he says, the very pinnacle of courtesy and patience.

She stares at him with her eyes narrowed for a moment, then smiles approvingly. I release a breath I had no idea I was even holding.

"I like this one, Serena," she tells me with a wink. "However! I do not like the fact that you have come charging in here with a gun while you're carrying my grandchild! Serena, you should know better than that! What if something had happened? What if the gun misfired? What if you fell down and injured yourself? What if—"

"Yes, I know, I know. Trust me, I don't plan on making a habit of it," I assure her, helping her into the back seat of the car. She crosses her legs and folds her hands in her lap, looking every bit as dignified and ladylike as she always does, even considering her ragged, dirty clothes and tangled hair. She's missing one shoe, too, I notice. But I figure that is absolutely not the best thing to mention at the moment.

As we drive back onto the highway, Luca looks at her in the rearview mirror, like he did to me not even twenty minutes ago.

"Mrs. De Laurentis, I know this may seem like an odd question, but I have to ask: I don't suppose there's any chance you might know where we could find Don Abruzzi, is there?"

I turn and look at her, waiting for some kind of snappy response.

Instead, she sighs heavily and rolls her eyes. "Ricky Abruzzi? I've known that little bastard since we were in grade school. I can tell you exactly where he lives. Hell, I can tell you things about that man you wouldn't believe."

Luca and I look at each other, smiling, as my mother tells us everything she knows.

DON ABRUZZI

"**I** assure you, it's real," I say, gesturing up to the lion's head mounted on my wall in one of the smoking rooms where some of my guests are lounging and drinking. "This one was from a hunt in Zimbabwe back in...I want to say '85? I was a younger man back then," I add with a laugh, and the handful of men looking at the trophy with me laugh politely with me.

We're about two hours into this little house party at one of my private homes outside the city, and it couldn't have come at a worse time.

The men standing around me, along with most of the guests, are some very important men of the Bronx. And in the next few weeks, they're going to become *the* most important men in the Bronx.

Most of them are men like me. Some of them come from other lesser mafia families that have been very reasonable in realizing that the Abruzzi family is the future of the Bronx. Some of them come from less organized parts of the city's underworld—there are the drug traffickers with their South American connections and taste for luxury and decadence, there are the smugglers who *deal with women,* and there are security contractors who provide mercenaries to men who need them.

Not everyone comes from that unsavory part of life, though. There are more than a few lawyers here, along with a few small-time local politicians, most of them already having mafia connections. Some of them are new faces, though.

There's an air of promise and a new future for my family in this house. It's a party I've been setting up for several months now, and it's going splendidly —which is why I *should* be having the time of my life.

Instead, an old thorn in my side is aggravating me.

Luca Lomaglio couldn't wait *one more week* to come back from the dead, could he? By the time I got word from my incompetent men that he was on his way back to New York, he must have already been halfway across the Atlantic. I hardly had time to get men looking for him before I got word the Costas had holed up in the fucking soap shop.

Once they're all dead, I'm going to have the place burned to the ground.

But business like that waits for no one, so I'm

having to wait for status updates on a fucking fire-fight in the streets while entertaining the men who are going to rule the Bronx under me in the next few years.

"Come on, Don Abruzzi," says Mr. Giudici, one of the biggest meth kingpins in the neighborhood, "I'm sure hunting lions wasn't the only thing you spent time doing down in Zimbabwe."

"Certainly not," I say, flashing him a smile. "There's an ivory statuette I need to show you in the gallery, if you remind me—and of course, there are some other exquisite things Africa has to offer." I lower my voice, even though my wife is long dead and not around to hear me say, "And the women you can acquire are like nothing you've ever experi-enced." Amid the chuckles from the men, I add, "Except, of course, what our friend Mr. Ghardesca can offer." I give a polite gesture to the man himself, one of the last major human traffickers in New York.

"I hope not to prove you wrong, Don Abruzzi," says Mr. Ghardesca, raising his glass of wine to me, and the rest of us raise our glasses briefly.

"Quite so, quite so," I chuckle.

Then I hear someone clear his throat behind me, and somehow, I know it's going to be bad news.

"Yes?" I ask, peering over my shoulder to see one of my capos standing there, phone in hand. "Is this important, Tom?"

"Valentino needs you to give him a call," he leans

in to say in a low enough tone that only I can hear him. "It's about the soap shop."

His face is glassy.

But I'm used to keeping myself composed, so I just turn to my guests and smile affably.

"Gentlemen, if you'll excuse me, I need to get some fresh air. In the meantime, Tom—get these good gentlemen a little food, it's been a bit since we've eaten. Some of the cigars too, and one for me when I get back."

"Yes, Don Abruzzi."

I take the burner phone from his hand and make my way out of the house into the back yard, and as soon as I'm out of sight of the other men, my jaw clenches.

I trudge down a little cobblestone path I had laid in my backyard leading down to a spacious gazebo that overlooks a large pond. It was one of the first things I had built when I bought this place, and it's become the place I go to when I need to make business calls. It's far enough from the house that nobody can hear me, and it's elegant enough that I don't look impolite as I would walking down the road out of sight.

I call Valentino, another one of my capos, and glare out onto the pond while I listen to the rings. He picks up almost immediately.

"Need this to be important, Val," I growl into the phone. "What's the situation at the soap shop?"

"That's the problem," his gruff voice says immediately. "Haven't gotten an update yet. Should be over by now."

My grip tightens on the phone, and I have to hold back the urge to hurl it into the pond and scream. I take a deep breath and try to focus myself.

"Do we have eyes on the ground over there?" I say, trying to get *some* intel out of him.

"Can't get a hold of anyone who hit the place," he says. "I've got men headed down there now to try to scope it out."

"They'd better have a fucking good reason for not checking in," I say pointedly, "and who the fuck was leading them? Jack, the Costa turncoat? Make sure that chickenshit isn't pulling anything stupid or I'll have his liver cut out, understand?"

There's silence for a few moments between us as I take a few breaths, pacing back and forth in the gazebo and wishing I had a cigarette in hand. Better yet, a little morphine.

"Luca Lomaglio was going to be at that soap shop, Val."

"Yes, boss."

"I need him dead, Val."

"Yes, boss."

"I'm done playing goddamn games with this," I say, rubbing my temple. "If they want to try to jerk us around, we jerk back. Execute Luisa De Laurentis, we don't need her anymore. I was gonna put a fucking bastard in her belly, but the bitch is probably too dried up down there to be of any use anyway."

Valentino doesn't reply.

"Val, don't you fucking get cold feet on me now," I say in a low hiss, careful not to look half as furious as I am from a distance, in case anyone's watching from the house. "If you don't do it, I'll come down there myself and personally put a bullet in the poor widow's goddamn heart right before I put one in yours."

"I can't get a hold of the men who have her, either," Valentino says in a muted tone.

My face goes pale.

One group not checking in is bad and could mean something *very* bad. But two groups going silent…

"Run that by me again, Val, I must be hard of hearing."

I hear a sigh from Val's end of the line, and I can almost see him running his hands through his hair nervously.

"We can't get a hold of anyone who's on the ground out there. I've already got men on the way to find out what's up with the De Laurentis widow, and-"

I hardly listen to everything else my capo rattles off to me. I'm leaning against the gazebo, rubbing my head as a throbbing headache starts blooming.

"Val?" I interrupt him after a few moments.

"Listen very carefully. A hell of a lot depends on Luca Lomaglio being dead and Luisa De Laurentis on her way to being dead. You've made it very clear that things are not ideal right now," I say tersely, "but you're a competent man. I have my hands full with these other...gentlemen...at this party. So I'm giving you free reign to spend whatever you need to make this problem go away. You do this for me, maybe I'll let you have a turn with Serena De Laurentis before we ship her off to the Russians, or wherever the fuck Ghardesca sends his women."

"Understood, Don Abruzzi," Valentino says, swallowing hard. Before he can say anything else, I end the call.

Just a few more hours, and I can clear the house out and give this the attention it deserves, I think to myself as I march back up to the house.

When I open the back door and step inside, the smell of Sicilian black wine being poured greets me, and I feel just a little of the stress melt away. I greet a few more people on my way through the kitchen, all smiles and handshakes, like we're all old friends just watching out for each other, like none of the ugly business we carry out is right under the surface.

It's the game we play in the mafia. We hug, we kiss each other on the cheek, and my subordinates kiss my hand before doing what I want them to do to keep our pockets lined with money. I was born into it, and it's been going on for hundreds of years before me.

I'll be damned if some punk-ass carpenter from Taranto fucks that all up for me.

But first, I could use a few of the oxy pills I have in the bathroom upstairs. As I navigate the party guests, I smile and politely excuse myself on my way to the fine wooden stairs to the second floor.

None of the guests are up here, so it gives me a little quiet comfort. No sounds but my footsteps and the ticking grandfather clock in the hallway leading to the master bedroom.

I run my hand through my hair as I enter it, crossing the massive bedroom with its four-poster bed and entering the grand bathroom, tiled with white marble and big enough to be a spare room of its own.

At the mirror, I glance at my face before reaching for the orange bottle of pills on the shelf. I pop a few of them into my hand...and I pause.

The hairs on the back of my neck stand on end.

I slowly lift my eyes back to the mirror, and my whole body goes still.

In the reflection, I see the doorframe behind me leading back to the bedroom.

Standing in the doorway is Luca Lomaglio.

"Hello, Ricky," his deep voice rumbles. He looks like he just came from a fight, yet he's calm as a statue. And there's a silenced pistol in his hand.

Fuck.

Staring him in the eye through the mirror, I take the pills dry before setting my hands on the sink to hold myself up. I stare at him for a few long, hard moments before speaking.

"So sorry, Luca," I say, keeping my voice calm but not hiding my hatred for him. "Your invitation must have gotten lost in the mail."

"Actually, I'm Lusia De Laurentis's plus-one," he says, tilting his head to the side with a cocky smile. "Might've gotten lost getting here without her help. She and her daughter say hello."

My mouth twists into a grimace.

A hundred thoughts go through my head at once, and then they all settle. Everything feels still, except for a singular hatred in my heart for the man in the doorway and everything he's done to my beautiful empire. I'm still looking at him through the mirror, and I don't know if I could tear my eyes away if I tried.

"Not a bad play," I admit at last. "You made yourself a legend, snuffed out my lineage, got yourself fucking a fertile piece of old mafia royalty, and got me in the one place where the Abruzzi family will never recover from. Shit, what are you, thirty? Not even that old? You don't even know who half the fuckers downstairs are, do you?"

A sick laugh comes from my chest.

"You might not have finesse, but I know skill

when I see it. You'll do well as don of your own family, Luca Lomaglio."

His face goes hard, and he narrows his eyes.

"Really? That's what you think this is about? You think I'm here to take your place and keep running this shitshow?" He shakes his head slowly. "I was raised by a carpenter. I grew up between one of the poorest towns in Italy and the poorest neighborhoods in NYC. I don't make *contacts*, Abruzzi, I make friends. I've made bonds that last. And we're all sick of this bullshit you're running. But most of all, you hurt the people I love, and you've hurt a lot more than that."

"You've gotta be kidding me," I laugh, turning around to face Luca. "Am I really about to get killed by someone who thinks he's doing good for the world? This isn't how we do things, you fucking boyscout. We do this because those of us who are better than the rest know how to handle ourselves. That could be you, but you're too fucking dense to see it. You think you're some kind of saint?"

"No," he says, cracking a smile, and he raises his pistol to my head. "A saint would let you live."

*B*oom!

The cork of the champagne bottle shoots up toward the ceiling, and Giovanni swears as he runs across the room to catch it, not spilling a drop of the bubbly liquid he just opened. Well, unless the foam gushing out the top counts.

"*Accidenti*, Giovanni, can't save it for the reception?" I shout at Giovanni in Italian as he catches the cork triumphantly, holding it up for the other groomsmen to see. "If you don't keep steady during the vows, I'll kick your ass."

We laugh, but honestly, I couldn't care less if he was trashed—this is the happiest day of my life, and nothing could change that.

I'm wearing a jet-black fitted tuxedo, minus the coat, and all the men are helping me get ready. Nico, my best man, is helping me with the bowtie in front of a large mirror.

"It's not for me," says Giovanni, "I've got a few bottles I'm gonna give out in glasses to the guests when they get here. Real fancy, I saw someone do it on TV."

Nico and I exchange a grin, and I catch sight of my dad chuckling behind me in the mirror.

"Well, what's one bottle among a few groomsmen? None for the groom, though—I've got a bottle of your mother's limoncello we're going to get into at the reception," he says, wagging a finger, and I grin at him.

My own wedding. I never thought I'd see this day in a million years, and I'm even more stunned that my parents are able to see it. My mom is off with Luisa fussing over Serena and helping her get ready.

The past few months have been a storm, though, and this may technically be the calm *after* the storm, the energy definitely hasn't settled down.

I killed Don Abruzzi that night. He wasn't the only monster in that household I dealt with that night, either. The whole of the Bronx's underworld took a massive hit thanks to me, and since then, the remnants of the Cleaners and their allies have been broken, weak, and driven into hiding.

Finally, definitively, the Cleaners are finished, and the last nail is in the Abruzzi coffin.

Abruzzi was right, too—if I wanted to, I could

step into this power vacuum and become the most feared man in this side of New York.

But that's not me. It never has been, and it never will be. I've gotten a taste of what it means to have family, to risk losing it, the joy of building it. It won't be too long before I'll know what it's like to raise one with Serena.

The thought makes my heart swell.

"Careful, Dad, these Americans might not have as much restraint as you," I say as Nico finishes with my bowtie and pats me on the shoulder.

"Damn, Luca, you clean up alright," Nico admits, admiring the outfit as I do the same.

"Yeah yeah, you had your chance with me," I joke with him, ribbing him in the side while he play-punches at me like we're a couple of boys fighting in the yard again.

My phone buzzes, and while I check it, my dad glances around at all the assembled men, some of them still getting their outfits ready while others like Giovanni...well, wander around making trouble.

I wouldn't have it any other way.

"Almost," I answer my dad after looking at my phone, grinning broadly. "Last one just showed up."

"Oh, another one of your friends?" he asks, and I nod for him to follow me.

"Someone you'll want to meet," I say, leading him to the door of the chapel. He follows me with a happy but confused face until I push the door open.

When he looks down the steps of the chapel, he looks like he's about to faint.

Uncle Carlo climbs out of a cab, leaning on a cane and giving a mile-wide grin up to my father.

"...Carlo," my father breathes, his voice weak. "Carlo!" Hurrying as much as an older man can, he hobbles down the stairs as my uncle's grin breaks into warm laughter, and as soon as the two men are together, they throw their arms around each other in a warm hug, their voices breaking as they laugh.

"*Mio fratello!*" Carlo nearly sobs into his brother's arms, and the two begin talking to each other in rapid Italian in low tones, their eyes as full of tears as of emotions.

News of Carlo's recovery had been a huge relief to all of us, but when I heard my parents could make it, I wanted to make sure the reunion was worthwhile and I managed to avoid the subject of Carlo and keep the surprise.

I was a little worried the surprise would give my dad a heart attack, but the two of them are more hardy than I was worried. They almost look young again.

Nico appears at my side. "Damn, you don't see the resemblance until they're together again, huh?"

"I know. They've lived worlds apart for a long time. They'll have...a great deal to catch up on," I say, putting it lightly and flashing Nico a smile. "Come on, let's leave them to it. We've got a wedding to finish setting up."

~

*E*ven though it's barely a couple hours later, it feels like an eternity of waiting, but at last, everyone is gathered together and ready for the ceremony as the music starts.

All across the room, faces are glowing with anticipation. The sides could hardly look more different, too. On the one side are Serena's family and friends. Of course, because of everything that happened with her father, it's only her mother's family that's represented, but they're all there and looking beautiful. Dark skin and light hair seems to run in the family, and they could practically be cousins to the other side of the family. My southern Italian family is on the swarthy side, and good god, are there a lot of them.

There are cousins and second cousins and third cousins, many with their families, thanks to me being able to help some of them over. Turns out I even have a few distant relatives already in America who immigrated separately. The whole chapel is as Italian-American as it could be.

Then the doors open, and I'm genuinely struck dumb as the music starts.

Serena looks downright angelic. Her dress is a

lovingly intricate pattern of lace at the top, and from the hips down the center of her legs, the pure-white fabric is smooth as fresh snow on a mountainside with two tresses of fluffier fabric down the sides of her legs like wispy clouds. Her beauty is ethereal, and the long golden hair curling down her shoulders is like a crown to it all.

But her face is what draws my attention. I've seen Serena's face through good times and bad times, lying beside her in bed and running from life-threatening danger. I've seen it weeping bitter tears, and I've seen it beaming with real, true happiness.

But when I look at it now, I see all that glowing bright in that one expression, bound up together. Of course, I can't help the stupid grin that crosses my face, and as she sees me, her face does the same.

Rafaela is her maid of honor, watching her approach proudly, and Nico on my side is nearly in tears. Luisa stands nearby, holding our newborn baby son, healthy and strong, who'll one day have the strength of his father and the courage and heart of his mother. Luisa's tears flow much more freely down her beaming smile.

I've heard some people say that watching your bride come down the aisle toward you is like seeing a new person, starting a new life with them as a new pair of people, building something from the ground up together.

With Serena coming toward me, I feel nothing like that.

I see the girl I fell in love with on that old construction site. I see the woman I reconnected with after what felt like a lifetime. I see the face that greeted me when I broke out of prison and endured so much without me. I see my lover, who fought to make it through a world that's been lined up against both of us since we were teenagers.

Soon, Serena is standing in front of me, her eyes wet with tears, and when I blink, I realize mine are too.

The minister doesn't even have to start speaking for us to know that we're already in this together forever—we always have been, through the good times and the easy times, and with all the worry and danger behind us at long last, nothing can shake that ever again.

We'll always be bound for life.

TWO YEARS LATER

"*Voglio giocare all'esterno*," I say very slowly, sitting on the porch with my two-year-old standing wobbly on my lap. I've been trying to teach him Italian alongside English, to surprise Luca's family when they come to visit in the summer.

"*Voglio... gio...* Daddy!" Matteo sounds out, exploding into giggles at the end of his 'sentence' when Luca comes walking up the driveway, returning from delivering one of his latest carpentry creations. Matteo starts bouncing and wiggling, waving his arms excitedly as he always does when Luca comes home.

My husband looks exhausted but happy, his muscles showing through his white T-shirt, smudges of oil and grime on his clothing.

He's been working as a carpenter from home,

building custom cabinets, armoires, sheds, even taking on jobs working on houses like he used to as a teenager. It's the kind of work he was made for—solitary, precise, intense. He knows how to take a customer's list of wants and needs and transform their dream into reality.

Luca is amazing at his job, getting customers from far and wide to drive all the way out to our teeny tiny little town on the outskirts of Ithaca, New York, not too far from the cabin where we once hid out together. It seems so long ago that our lives were that way—scary, uncertain, always changing.

Nowadays, things are simple. We work with our hands—Luca builds things, I've turned Bathing Beauty into a lucrative online bath goods shop, shipping my luxurious creations all over the country. We grow things in our garden, using knowledge I picked up during my time at the women's shelter in Italy. Luca even built our house, almost entirely by himself, by hand.

Shortly before the baby was born, the house was finished, and we moved in just in time.

A week later, before all our boxes were even fully unpacked, Matteo was born healthy and huge. On the phone, Luca's mother did warn me that Luca was a heavy baby, but I guess I just never expected Matteo to turn out to be as big and strong as his father.

I'm grateful, though.

Matteo has his father's size and his beautiful green eyes, and he has my dark-blond hair and button nose. He's in his terrible twos right now, but if I'm being perfectly honest, he's about as far from terrible as it gets. He's a little rowdy sometimes, but when I think about how Luca apparently was as a young kid, it's no surprise that he would inherit those genes. I'm ready for it, though. All of it.

"How is my beautiful wife this afternoon?" Luca asks as he walks up and bends down to kiss me. Matteo blows raspberries, shaking his head at how gross his parents are.

"I'm wonderful. What did we do while you were gone… oh, yeah. We picked some tomatoes and we read a couple of books, didn't we, Matteo?"

Our son nods and reaches for Luca, who scoops him up and swings him around, making him laugh.

"Sounds like a great time," Luca says, kissing Matteo on the cheek.

"How did the delivery go? Did they love their new coffee table?" I ask, getting up to follow Luca into the house. He sets Matteo down in the living room and immediately the two-year-old goes running off down the hallway, yelling about how he's going to show us his favorite toy car. Never mind the fact that he's shown us this car every day for the past week.

Luca grins.

"They loved it. Mrs. Harris, you know the older

lady who ordered it, she actually cried when she saw it. Can you believe that?"

"Well, you're very good."

"It's a coffee table," he says, laughing. "But as long as they're happy tears, I'm fine."

Just then, my phone buzzes in my pocket and I pull it out to read a message from Rafaela. I grin and type out a response.

"That Rafaela?" Luca asks.

"Yep. She said she switched some shifts around and got her patients covered, so she is for sure going to be available the whole week to come up and watch Matteo for us," I announce happily.

"Phew. Crisis averted. I doubt your mom would survive a week up here in the woods to watch him," Luca jokes. And he's right. I mean, she would suck it up and deal with it, but my mother is absolutely not the outdoorsy type. She'd be missing her bi-weekly manicure and constant French cuisine delivery very quickly.

"Aunt Raf?" Matteo chirps, suddenly toddling back into the kitchen.

I stifle a giggle. Matteo is honestly a little obsessed with his Aunt Raf. At first I was a little worried when Luca and I started planning this road trip across America, thinking Matteo would feel left out. But I know once Rafaela gets here, he'll be so distracted playing with her and Nico that he'll hardly even notice we're gone.

And with all the hectic life changes of the past couple years—getting married, moving up to Ithaca, having Matteo, settling into our new jobs—we haven't had a chance to have a real romantic getaway, just the two of us. The timing is perfect, landing right around our anniversary, and even though it will be difficult being away from Matteo for a whole week, we're looking forward to it.

Besides, Rafaela has been begging us to let her babysit for longer than a day or two. She and Nico are trying to get pregnant, and they could use all the childcare practice they can get.

"Did you get the confirmation for our reservation at that fancy hotel in San Francisco?" I ask Luca, scooping Matteo up into my arms and booping him on the nose.

"Yes. They want to know what time we'll be checking in, but I'll email them with the details later," Luca says, opening the refrigerator and pulling out a bottle of wine. "So, what are we thinking for dinner? You feel like cooking or do you want me to pick up some pizza?"

"Hmm. I'll cook if you want to keep Matteo busy," I tell him, eyeing the bottle of wine. "Oh! I almost forgot: you'll never guess who I heard from today."

"Who?"

"Francesca!" I exclaim, still giddy with the news. "She said she's been doing really well. She finally moved out of that awful apartment and got a place down by the beach."

"Whoa, *e fantastico*," he says, genuinely impressed. Francesca's had some rough times trying to get settled, balancing being a single mother to her daughter, Luciana, and finding full-time work. But recently, she met a guy who's been treating her very well. I'm so happy for her.

"Yeah, she's still helping out with the shelter, of course. She said everyone there is doing well, too, but they miss me," I add.

"Well, as soon as Matteo is big enough to handle such a major trip, we'll go visit. My parents are dying to have us stay with them again. I think they really just want my opinion on the new guy Domenica's been seeing, though," Luca says, chuckling. "One of these days, they'll understand that whatever Domenica wants, Domenica gets. She's just as stubborn as I am."

"Yeah, there's a lot of that going on in this family," I remark cheekily.

"Hmm. I'll never get tired of hearing that," he says.

"What?" I ask, reaching for the bottle to pour myself a glass of wine.

"*Family.* Sometimes I still can't believe how lucky I am," Luca explains. I set Matteo back down and walk over. Luca folds me in his arms and kisses me. Softly, but with passion.

"Me neither. It feels like a dream," I tell him, grinning.

"But better than a dream," he says. "Because it's real."

~

Thank you so much for reading! I hope you enjoyed this trilogy <3 If you have a moment, please leave a review. Other readers are dying to know what you thought.

I have plenty more bad boy romance for you, so make sure you check out my other books on the next couple of pages, and sign up for my newsletter to be notified when I have a new release on the way!

~Alexis Abbott

TRANSLATIONS

ITALIAN

Passerotta mia – my sparrow (term of endearment)

biglietto – ticket

volo – fly

prezzo – price

dolcezza – sweetie

accidenti – damn

salute – cheers

vendetta – revenge

grazie per l'aiuto – thanks for the help

non dovevi farlo – you didn't have to do that

stronzo – fucker

orrendo – horrible

bene – good

fratello – brother

informatore – informant/spy

carissima – dearest one
sei tu – is it you
vieni – come
mio figlio – my son
chi sei – who are you
la mia bella sorella – my beautiful sister
e possibile – is it possible
Papa, sono io – Dad, it's me
veramente – truly
brava ragazza – good girl

SPANISH

hermana – sister
  amiga – friend (female)

ALSO BY ALEXIS ABBOTT

Romantic Suspense:

HITMEN SERIES:

Owned by the Hitman

Sold to the Hitman

Saved by the Hitman

Captive of the Hitman

Stolen from the Hitman

Hostage of the Hitman

Taken by the Hitman

The Hitman's Masquerade (Short Story)

THE KILLER TRILOGY:

Book 1: Killer for Hire

Book 2: Killer Desire

Book 3: Killer on Fire

SEXY SEALs

Sweetheart for the SEAL

Sights on the SEAL

HOSTAGES:

Stealing Her

The Assassin's Heart

Killing For Her

Abducted

Stepbrothers:

Ruthless

Criminal

Standalones:

Betting on Love

Hunter's Baby

I Hired A Hitman

Vegas Boss

Rock Hard Bodyguard

Innocence For Sale: Jane

Redeeming Viktor

<u>Romance:</u>

Falling for her Boss (Novella)

Most Wanted: Lilly (Novella)

Bound as the World Burns (SFF)

<u>Erotic Thriller:</u>

The Dangerous Men Series:

The Narrow Path

Strayed from the Path

Path to Ruin

ABOUT THE AUTHOR

Alexis Abbott is a Wall Street Journal & USA Today bestselling author who writes about bad boys protecting their girls! Pick up her books today if you can't resist a bad boy who is a good man, and find yourself transported with super steamy sex, gritty suspense, and lots of romance.

She lives in beautiful St. John's, NL, Canada with her amazing husband.

facebook.com/abbottauthor

twitter.com/abbottauthor

instagram.com/alexisabbottauthor

bookbub.com/authors/alexis-abbott

pinterest.com/badboyromance

youtube.com/AlexisAbbott

ACKNOWLEDGMENTS

Thank you to my amazing Patrons. I'm constantly humbled and grateful for your support.

Ramona Cabrera
Melissa Hedrick
Virginia Swanson
Dawn Daughenbaugh
Don Doss
Stacie Currie

If you'd like to join them — and get my ebooks or paperbacks — you can find me here on Patreon.
https://www.patreon.com/alexisabbott